T0354793

CAVES, THE UNKNOWN & THE WILL

CAVES, THE UNKNOWN & THE WILL

PASTOR TORRES

CAVES, THE UNKNOWN & THE WILL

iUniverse books may be ordered through booksellers or by contacting:

iUniverse
1663 Liberty Drive
Bloomington, IN 47403
www.iuniverse.com
844-349-9409

ISBN: 978-1-6632-6324-7 (sc)
ISBN: 978-1-6632-6325-4 (e)

Library of Congress Control Number: 2024910557

Print information available on the last page.

iUniverse rev. date: 09/25/2024

THE AUTHOR

PASTOR M TORRES WAS BORN IN HAVANA, CUBA. HE GRADUATED FROM THE SCHOOL OF MEDICINE IN HAVANA AND CURRENTLY RESIDES IN MIAMI, FLORIDA WHERE HE PRACTICES MEDICINE.

HIS INTEREST IN SPELEOLOGY WAS FOUNDED THROUGH HIS PARTICIPATION IN: SOCIEDAD ESPELEOLOGICA DE CUBA, GRUPO DE EXPLORACIONES CIENTIFICAS, GRUPO PEDRO BORRAS.

AMONG OTHER PUBLISHED WORKS IN SPELEOLOGY INCLUDE:

1961 FINDING THE HISTOPLASMA CAPSULATUM IN PAREDONES CAVE. GEC MAGAZINE, HAVANA, CUBA

1970 THE CAVE OF SANTA ACADEMY OF SCIENCE, INSTITUTE OF GEOGRAPHY, HAVANA, CUBA

1972 PALEOPATOLOGY OF THE CUBAN ABORIGINES. ACADEMY OF SCIENCE. INSTITUTE OF GEOGRAPHY, HAVANA, CUBA.

1973 PRELIMINARY STUDY OF THE CAVE OF FUENTES. ACADEMY OF SCIENCE, INSTITUTE OF GEOGRAPHY, HAVANA, CUBA.

CAVES, THE UNKNOWN & THE WILL

ONE OF FICTION'S PURPOSES IS TO
CONCEAL THE TRUTH.
PASTOR TORRES

CAVES, THE UNKNOWN & THE WILL

AUTHOR: PASTOR TORRES

Register of Copyrights, Unites States of America:
TXu 1-572-943 – August 15, 2007

CAVES, THE UNKNOWN & THE WILL

> One of fiction's purposes is to conceal the truth.
> Pastor Torres

MIAMI, FLORIDA. Any given day.

Dr. Torres, a Cuban surgeon presently living in Miami, gets a phone call.

- Hello? Who is this? Andy! I haven't heard from you in twenty years! How are you?

After many greetings and surprises and even though they are on opposite sides of politics, the old friendship between them is stronger than their differences and they start remembering their many adventures in Cuba.

- So you are passing through Miami on your way to Puerto Rico for a Speleological conference. Where are you staying?

- At my uncle's house, responds Andy.

- What is the address?

Andy gives him the address. It is Downtown Miami.

- OK, I will pass by tomorrow at around 11 AM. I want you to come have lunch at our house.

THE BEGINNING

THE NEXT DAY I STOP BY TO PICK UP ANDY AND WE HEAD TO MY home. My wife and old expedition companion, Miriam, is waiting for us. After lunch and a couple of Cuban coffees, we finally sat down to talk about old times of speleological and archeological explorations.

- So how have you been? – I asked Andy.

- Well, I am still working in the same place. You know that Speleology is my life. I now have much more responsibilities since Antonio, as you may know, is not doing very well. He has heart problems. By the way, I brought you some of his books in which there are a couple of Pictures of you and some mention of your various works.

I thank him, as I had no idea the books even existed.

The conversation goes on for hours.

I ask him for Pio Domingo, a cavern on the occidental part of Cuba. He tells me that nobody is allowed to enter that area, as it is now a government base. (Seems to be so secretive that not even they can go by). In that same military zone is also El Hoyo del Potrerito.

I don't say anything but I wonder to myself what they are doing to my favorite cavern of Pio Domingo. El Hoyo del Potrerito, at the Sotorraneos Cavern, in Cueva Oscura, Cueva Clara, El Sumidero of the Guyaguateje river. All of them are in the same area we walked and explored years ago along with the Pedro A. Borras group, a specialized unit in Speleology where we were all members. Are they now destroying everything?

His voice brings me back to reality. He goes on to tell me how they are now doing Speleological tours, with tourists from all over the world. He also says that, if we are willing, we can go whenever we want. He goes on to assure me that there will be no problem whatsoever and tells me to call him so he can prepare everything for us and send us a formal invitation to visit the different Speleological zones.

    —   Could we visit the Fuentes Cavern? – I ask.

    —   Of course! – He replies.

Time passes. After taking some pictures and saying goodbye to Miriam, I took him back to his uncle's house.

I didn't see him again for a few months, when he came by on his way to New York where he would be attending a meeting at the Smithsonian Institute and then visiting some Indian reservations on the Canadian border.

This time we got together at a restaurant for dinner and we spoke of old friends, to whom he said he told about our encounter a few months before. He also told me about Antonio's death. Antonio was the Director of the Science Institute.

He brought me a couple of books and some pictures of the whole group, including myself, of the times when, back in the 60s, our lives revolved around the exploration of Cuban caverns. I talk to him again about the Pio Domingo cavern and the Picapica valley but I cannot get him to give me any new information.

He insists on telling me that, should I decide to travel to Cuba, we could go on an expedition accompanied by some local Speleologists. The idea of the other Speleologists would be with the purpose to preserve the caverns and also to help us stay safe. I would dare to say what they really want is to watch our every step.

Among other things, he tells me about Fidel Castro's poor health, and explains that there is high concern about this and about what could happen if he were to die.

I take him back to his family's home, this time in the Kendall area and after saying our goodbyes, I start to drive home. I cannot stop thinking about everything we have talked about and a thought comes into my mind...Something that has lived with me for many years and that I have not been able to forget...not even after my many years in exile.

I cannot get any sleep tonight!

THE DECISION

MAY 2007

It's early morning, I've made a decision. I pick up my phonebook and I start going through it. The first name I see is Norman, retired engineer and exceptionally brilliant. Norman has been a friend since high school. After some fruitless calls, I reach him in New Jersey. We exchange hellos and I tell him what my plans are, these reawake his adventurous spirit (something he has never lost). We arrange to meet in Miami on May 7th.

Next name on the list is John, ex marine and a good friend for the past fifteen years. I reach him on his boat – he is fishing in the Bahamas. We agreed to meet in two days, upon his return to Fort Lauderdale, at his house where he invites Miriam and me over to savor some fresh fish.

Two days later, during a rainy afternoon, we arrived at John's house. We park on the driveway in front of an ample, beautiful house with access to a canal. Towards the back, next to the dock, we see John's 40 foot Viking. Miriam and I walk to the front door and ring the doorbell and just a couple of minutes later, John's wife, Mary, greets us. After the usual cordial greetings, we walk towards the family room just as John closes the sliding doors to the patio keeping the dogs away from us.

    –   How are you? How is fishing? – I ask John.

4

- It's quite good. You'll see for yourself once you taste the Dorado I caught. Are you hungry? Let's eat and then we'll talk.

After a hearty meal, along with some good tasting California White wine, we go to the den to have some American coffee. While sitting on a wicker sofa, John looks at me and asks:

- So Doc, what brings you here? That phone call of yours and this sudden visit has me wondering. I have a weary feeling.

I smile. Mary & Miriam get up to go to the kitchen to prepare the coffee and look over some souvenirs they've brought back from the Bahamas.

- So tell me, what's up? – John insists.

- John – I said – You're going to think I'm crazy for what I'm about to tell you. I've known you for many years and I know you like these types of things. Besides, it's for a good cause and I can also trust you.

- What is it? – John asks.

- We have to penetrate Cuba with explosives.

- You're crazy Doc!

- I knew you were going to say that but it's not what you think. It's not to overthrow Castro's regime. We need to excavate a cavern to look for something. I cannot tell you what it is now, but it's something very valuable and we don't want it to fall into the hands of Castro's regime. For more than thirty years, I've kept this secret but I've received alarming news. I must act even though it might sound like an insane idea.

— So, we have to go to Cuba with explosives? – John asks.

— Yes, but not all of us need to enter the island with explosives. – I answer.

— As you may well know, there is some tolerance now by the Cuban government about traveling to the island. However, you won't be able to travel directly because of the restrictions of the US government. But then again, we only need a few men to bring in the equipment undercover. The rest can be brought in through customs.

— What would you need? -Asks John.

— If we are caught, we will be executed. Therefore, we are going to need some firearms to defend ourselves and a team of men we can trust. Well-trained men and only you know how to train them. One of them must be trained in demolition, another in communications. We will need some for backup and a few for our return trip via helicopter. -

— That is *if* we make it back. When would we leave? – John asks.

— As soon as you get the team together. We will get the Cuban passports and all the paperwork to enter the island. Our cover will be that of a scientific mission. That will also facilitate getting the permits from the US Government to travel. I think everything can be ready in a couple of months.

— You guys only need the US Passport. The covert team needs nothing.

— You're wrong, says John, they need to have balls!

- OK, let's meet in a month or two to meet the men and see what is needed. Here is a check to get you going. I knew I could count on you.

Today I've told Miriam that we are going to Cuba.

MAY 7TH

Norman shows up at my office in full camouflage. Half-bald and blue eyed, he looks more like a red neck than a Cuban.

- What's with the camouflage get up? – I ask.

- It's very comfortable and my neighbors in Alabama have no idea I'm Cuban.

- Ok, I still have a lot of work to do and it's only three o'clock. Here I'll jot down my home address. I'll see you there at eight. I picked up the phone to call Miriam. I let her know we are having a guest for dinner.

Norman shows up at eight sharp. We have a scrumptious Cuban dinner: black beans, white rice, fried plantains and roasted pig, along with some Chilean red wine. After savoring our Cuban coffee, we go and sit by the pool. Watching the moonlight reflecting on the water, I break the ice.

- Well I'll tell you why I asked you over. It's something I think you're going to like, more so now that you're not too busy.

- Tell me. – Norman says.

- We want to go to Cuba. – I answer.

- For what?

— It's a very long story. We'll have time to tell you about it later, but the important thing is we are going to go to Cuba to get something I found more than thirty years ago and now there is the danger that it might fall into communist hands.

— What? – Says a wide-eyed Norman.

— Being that you are a brilliant engineer, you're the one we need for this mission. It's risky but you'll love it and it's worthwhile.

— How so? – He asks.

— We have everything planned; we will enter the island as members of a scientific mission. Do you have your Cuban passport?

— Yes.

— Some of the other men will enter as tourists. Others will enter covertly. They will bring in the equipment we need.

— And what is it that we need?

— Explosives. Firearms.

— You're nuts.

— I knew you were going to say that. We need the explosives to find what we are looking for and maybe even to destroy it. The firearms are to defend ourselves, to escape in the event they discover what we are doing.

— This is very risky. – Norman says.

— We've done many dangerous things before. I guarantee you won't be disappointed.

— I'm not too sure but I'm intrigued. Now I am curious...I have to know. I think I'll bite the bait.

— I knew you would.

— I'm going to order all the speleological gear we will need. Hanging lamps, tents etc. Norman, you figure out what you will need on your side. There'll be a need to work with some complicated computer systems. Oh! And don't forget a radiation detector.

— I'm more intrigued by every passing moment. – Norman says.

— Do you remember the radiation detector you built for us more than thirty years ago? – I ask.

— Of course I remember but now it's easier to buy one!

— Well, don't forget to bring one.

After talking a bit longer we decide to meet in a couple of months to finalize the all the details of the trip

DOMINICAN
REPUBLIC

JUNE 1ST

WE HAVE A WHOLE WEEK OF VACATION TIME. MIRIAM AND I PACK our bags and fly out to the Dominican Republic. Our daughter, Yanet joins us. We arrived early at the Puerto Plata Hotel.

While at the hotel, I take some time out to make some calls. I call Alex, a retired doctor who is an old friend living in Santiago de los Caballeros. There is no answer. Apparently, there is no one home, so we decided to take a ride in our rented car to Sosua. Once we are there we stroll the streets where we come upon the first synagogue built by the first Jewish immigrants during World War II.

We keep on walking looking for a place called Cabarete, where there are some caverns. Finally we get there but it's too late. We decided to return the next day. That same night I tried in vain to contact Alex once more. Next morning we are tourists again and visit the caverns at Cabarete located deep within a forest. The caverns there have streaming water. One of them has a subterranean lake in which Yanet decides to take a swim.

That night I reached Alex. Tomorrow we will go and see him and have a chat with him.

The next morning, all three of us embarked on a trip. An hour and a half later and after asking for directions, we reached the house.

We knock at the door and Alex himself opens the door. He is his youthful self, greeting us with a joke. We sit down with Alex as his wife prepares a cup of Cuban coffee.

Alex starts of the conversation with a question:

- So what brings you here so unexpectedly?

- I tried calling you but didn't get an answer. Besides, I wanted to surprise you. How are things here with you? I answer.

- Good, things are good. The best part about living here is that there is no stress!

- Let me tell you, I'm planning a trip to Cuba in the coming months and I may be visiting Guantanamo. Do you still have family or any close friends there? (Alex was born in Guantanamo)

He says yes. He has family and some very good friends there.

- Let me give you their names and phone numbers in case you do go.

He takes a piece of paper and jots down the names and phone numbers of his brother and two close friends.

- These people are trustworthy. – He says – Contact them if you need anything. You can trust them as you trust me. I'm in contact with them. I'll let them know you might be coming.

We talked and exchanged jokes a while longer before deciding to go have dinner at a local restaurant, right in front of the monument that marks the center of the city. After a hefty meal of "mofongo" and some delicious coffee, we head back to the house. We say our goodbyes and head back to Puerto Plata.

During our ride back, Miriam is a little concerned.

- Guantanamo is at the other end of where we are planning to go in Cuba. What are we going to do there?

- Just in case. – I answer – If the helicopter fails, we need another route to escape. Remember that is where the Guantanamo Naval Base is.

MIAMI - SOMETHING UNEXPECTED

Upon our return from the Dominican Republic, I go back to my regular activities. One morning, while performing an operation at the Palm Springs Hospital (in Miami), I was having a conversation with Dr. Hassan, an anesthesiologist, about an art gallery he owns at Miami's famous eight street. During our conversation the name of a painter with strong ties to Cuba came up and Dr. Hassan invited me to come to meet him. I accepted and agreed to stop by the gallery in a couple of days, setting the time at 8 PM. As arranged, I arrived at the gallery at 8 PM sharp, after having somewhat of a hassle finding a parking space and walking half a block. I was amazed at the huge turn out of art enthusiasts and artists. I made my way over to Dr. Hassan, threw the crowd and congratulated him on the successful event. He pointed out some paintings, talked about the artists and introduced me to some of them. Then we came upon a long white haired man and he said:

- This is Pedro, the painter I told you about.

We shook hands and proceeded to engage in a long conversation about art. Then we spoke about archeology and as usual with any Cuban, we also funnily discussed politics. It was getting late, so I invited him and Dr. Hassan to have lunch the next day at a local restaurant called "El Versailles". They both readily agreed and we arranged to meet the next day at 11:00 AM.

Miriam joined me that day and at 11:00 AM sharp, we arrived at the restaurant. Dr. Hassan and Pedro met us at the door. We greeted each other and walked in. They seated us at a table in the back of the room and each one picked out a different dish. There is a lot to pick from Cuban cuisine.

During the conversation, Pedro spoke about some friends who belonged to human rights organizations and some that were renowned dissidents. I told him I was planning to go to Cuba on a scientific venture and that I was waiting for the US government approval to travel to the island. This last comment sparked his interest and lowering his voice he asked:

— Are you working with the CIA?

— No! – I said.

I explained that we had no ties to any government agencies but that we knew some top officials. I was lying but I wanted to know if he had any information.

— I would like to talk to you in private. – He said.

— Of course. Just tell me where and when? – I answered.

— Tomorrow at the gallery. Hassan has an office there. We can talk without problems.

— OK, we'll meet tomorrow then.

I was tied up at work so I got there somewhat late. When I got to the gallery, I found Pablo at the front door. He looked nervous.

— I thought you weren't coming!

I explained why I was late. That seemed to calm him some and we went into the back of the gallery where we found Hassan talking to some artist. I said hello and told him we were going to use the office to which he remarked:

— Sure. Use it as long as you want.

We entered the small office and sat down. Pedro looked at me and said:

— I am going to tell you something that you may find interesting.

— What is it? – I asked.

— I have a friend who's a dissident that sent me a note that's got me worried. You know about Castro's health. You know it's a military secret.

— Yes, I know. – I answered.

— Well this dissident has a friend who is a high-ranking official in Cuba. This Cuban official would like to contact someone of his own rank here in the USA. The guy has some important information. However, since he would be risking his life and that of his own family, he wants guaranteed asylum and money. What do you think?

— I don't know, it's above me. But I will try to contact someone and I will get back to you. – I said.

— Call Hassan. He will give me your message. I see him everyday.

— OK, I will let you know as soon as I can. – I answered.

On my way back, I called John. I asked him if he could stop by my office the next day. He says he can.

Next day John shows up at my office. My secretary sends him in immediately. I close the door to my office and tell him about the conversation I had with Pedro the day before.

— What do you think? – I ask.

— Very interesting, but what does that have to do with us?

— Come on John! You know I'm aware of your ties with the CIA and since we are going to Cuba anyway, ask some of your contacts if they would authorize us to find out if there is any truth to what Pedro said. If they do, then we will find out the name of the Cuban official or who the contact is. – I answered.

— Ok. I'll give you a call tomorrow.

He got up and left and I returned to work.

The morning after, just as I was about to leave, the phone rang. It was John.

— What's the word? – I asked.

— Lead them on. Find out who the contact is.

— Thanks. I will let you know when I have something.

That same morning I bumped into Dr. Hassan at the hospital. I tell him:

— I need you to tell Pedro that everything is going as planned. I will see him tomorrow at your gallery.

I arrived at the gallery at night the next day and found an enthusiastic Pedro waiting for me.

- Let's go into the office so you can tell me what you have. – He said.

- Where is Hassan? – I asked.

- He went for some Cuban coffee at Versailles restaurant. He'll be right back.

We stepped into the office and I told him I had contacted a CIA official and that we had the green light.

- Now Pedro, who is this Cuban official? – I asked.

- I don't know. The one that knows is Pepe, the dissident I told you about. He doesn't have a telephone but I'll give you his address. He lives in Lawton on Armas Street, in front of the park next to Porvenir Street. Everyone knows him as the crazy painter.

- Is that all you've got? – I asked.

- Well, you'll have to talk to him for more, I'll send him a note telling him you will be contacting him.

- Ok, I'll see what I can do. – I answered.

I said goodbye and as I was leaving Hassan arrived. I said goodbye to him also. On my way back home, all I could think of was how I was going to find out what was missing in the puzzle. That same night I sent an EMail to one of Miriam's family members who coincidentally lived near the alleged contact, Pepe.

Next day I got an answer. Pepe is for real. We've located him.

I pick up the phone, call John, and tell him everything is going as planned. Everything is under control.

JUNE 20TH

Today is the day when the team will meet at my house at 8 o'clock..

The first to arrive was John with Mary. We sat down in the living room and Mary, discreet as always, left us alone and went to chat with Miriam.

- I'm waiting for a friend to arrive. I want you to meet him. – I told John.

- What have you been up to? – John asks.

- Well, we have the Cuban Passports we will need to enter the Island and I've made some contacts in Cuba and I have managed to arrange a tour by the Cuban government of all the places we are interested in.

- What about you? – I ask John.

- The guys are ready. – He answers – Bill is an explosives expert, Tommy a communications expert, has all the equipment ready. Ben and Hans, warfare experts. We have some AK's, handguns etc. There will be five of us in total. We also have Charles and Jeff, ex marines. Experts in covert operations. I've also made contact with two pilots living in the Keys. They have two helicopters.

It's 8:30, there is a knock at the door. It's Norman.

- What's up? Says Norman as he walks towards me.

- Doing good – I answer – This is John, he is like a brother to me and he is going to head the team inside Cuba.

They shook hands and spent the rest of the evening talking. Before calling it a night, we agreed to meet in a week with the whole team. The departure date is set for July 22nd. We say our goodnights at the door.

JULY 1ST

Time seems to fly. All we can think about is the trip. We can't get a good night's sleep. We've contacted Miriam's family in Lawton, Havana, and some friends in San Jose de las Lajas. They are all awaiting our arrival at the end of the month. I also spoke on the phone with Andy. I've made arrangements with him and explained that our plan is to go with six speleologists. Five American tourists, Norman, Miriam and I who are the only Cuban born traveling. Our objective is to go to Pinar del Rio, a province on the western side of Cuba. Specifically to the Luis Lazo Valley so we can explore the Fuentes cavern.

I spend what's left of the month talking to my patients, getting family members names, numbers and addresses all at strategic points throughout the island.

I spoke to Marta today. She gave me her father's address. He lives just across the bridge that leads to the entrance of Varadero in the Matanzas province. He has a small abandoned farm in Varadero, specifically in Camarioca, which is close to the Cepero cavern, that would make a good hiding place and it is near the coast of the US. It's a place from where many Cuban rafters have embarked from in their desperate attempt to flee Cuba.

JULY 10TH

John called me today. The team is ready. They are staying at his house. Everything is a go. They are only waiting for Norman to arrive.

JULY NTH

Norman arrived at my house with a huge piece of luggage.

- Don't worry about anything – He says – I have anything we need, including the radiation detector.

- Ok! – I answer – You'll stay here at my house. Our meeting is set for the 15th to discuss the last details.

JULY 15TH

We are meeting with the whole team tonight. John arrives at eight with four of his guys: Bill, Tommy, Ben and Hans.

- Are they all here? – I ask.

- No – He answers – Charles and Jeff are on their way.

A while later our conversation is interrupted by a knock at the door. Charles and Jeff have arrived. The team is complete. We are a total of ten.

THE PLAN

JOHN CALLS THE MEETING TO ORDER IN AN AUTHORITATIVE VOICE and asks for silence. We are about to go into the details of the trip. John uses a blackboard he has brought with him and a slide projector. He begins his presentation:

– As you are all aware, this trip might have no return, if any of you have any doubts, now is the time to abandon the project.

There is total silence.

John goes on:

– Ok. According to our military code, from now on no one can leave. We are all aware of what the price of our decision might be. So, let's start. From this moment on, I will be the military leader of this operation. This assignment has been given to me by Dr. Torres. He himself will be in charge of intelligence. Charles will lead the infiltration team. Bill will take care of the explosives and Tommy will take care of communications. We had originally planned to leave on the 22nd, but we will now leave on the 20th. Dr. Torres, Miriam and Norman will leave on the 20th on a direct flight to Havana from Miami International Airport on a charter plane. They will be in Havana to greet us on the 24th.

– Bill, Tommy, Ben, Hans and I will leave on a flight to Cancun, Mexico on the morning of the 23rd. From there, we will fly to Havana on the 24th via Cubana de Aviación, the Cuban owned airline. The infiltration team will leave on the 24th. They will wait for orders in a safe house near the airport in the Florida Keys. They will have to be ready to leave on the spot since once the order is received, a speedboat will pick them up and drop them off six miles off the coast of Pinar del Rio province, directly north of Santa Lucia. They will use the Jutia lighthouse. This lighthouse has an embankment. Here they will unload the equipment and silent motors. They will have to disembark between 3 and 4 in the morning and cross the road that leads to the lighthouse embankment. Once there, they will hide in the forest until we pick them up that same day in the afternoon. Dr. Torres, please explain to them what that part of the country is like.

I get up and draw the province of Pinar del Rio on the blackboard, highlighting the port of Santa Lucia.

– Here – I say pointing to the blackboard – is a bay that was used to export copper from the Matahambre mine. We have been informed that mine is now closed so there is no activity on the bay. It is only used by some fishermen. You have to be very careful they don't notice your presence. I believe that in the early morning hours there will be no problem. After crossing the Guane road to your right, you must go deep into the jungle. Once there, go to the left. There is a farm that belongs to the state called Sarmiento.

Remember that the state police will be patrolling the port and the people's defense committee will be patrolling everyone inside the township. You must avoid the people of the town and stay within the darkness of the jungle. Bury all equipment near the road; make them accessible to be recovered by a jeep. Take cover somewhere far from it. The two inflatable rafts must be deflated and hidden near the coast. If you disembark at 3:00 AM, you only have one and a half hours to complete the plan. The backpacks with the explosives must be the first thing you hide, the firearms last, except your own. The government owned farm is used to sow rice so you will find flooded zones that will be difficult to cross. Any questions?

— How will we know when we will be picked up?

— Tommy will give you all radios with earpieces that way you will be able to hear us and contact us only in an extreme emergency. Never speak names or positions since there is a Chinese base near that can pick up communications. These radios are voice activated. They deactivate automatically. We will only use isolated words, always one minute after each half hour on the hour. Understood?

— OK – was answered in unison.

— John will give you word and numeric codes. Learn them. Remember not to have any identification with your. If anyone is captured, you are to say that you are fishermen and your boat sunk. Give a false name and ask to speak to your embassy. John's team will arrive at Jose Marti airport in the morning on the 24th. We are not sure how punctual the Cuban airliners are but I will be waiting for you. There will be a government official with me and some undercover government agents that will pretend not to understand English so it is absolutely prohibited to speak anything that can compromise us.

— You know nothing about military operations; you have not been members of the armed forces of this or any other country. You are only interested in speleology, mountaineering and nature. Be warned not to be tempted by prostitutes. Stay grouped together. If you have any doubts, call John or call me. If you need translators, call Norman, Miriam or me. Here are some magazines on speleology and mountaineering. Get familiar with both topics. We will have another meeting tomorrow so we can familiarize you with the geography and history of the zone we will be at and the geography of Cuba itself so you can place yourself and find possible escape routes.

JULY 16TH

It is sundown and everyone has arrived early at my house. It's almost 7pm. They are anxious to know all the details. We group at the living room around a small table where I have placed a projector.

—   There is no time to lose – I say to John while turning on the projector – The first slide projected is of the island of Cuba.

Signaling with a laser pointer, I tell them:

—   We are going to arrive here, in the province of Havana. From here, we will travel by the main highway to the province of Pinar Del Rio. From there we will continue on a narrow and treacherous road to the town of Sumidero. This small town is located at kilometer 32nd, which is marked on the road and ends at the town of Guane. If things have not changed, from there on it is all embankments until San Antonio Cape, where the island of Cuba ends. Beyond there, separated by about 131 miles, is the Yucatan stretch, Mexico.

—   Getting back to the town of Sumidero – I explain to them while changing the slide – we have another northward road that passes through the valley of Pica Pica. In it, is the Clara cavern on the Cuyaguateje river of Sumidero.

—   This area is restricted to us and it has been strictly militarized. It is top secret. Therefore, you must not even mention it even if you hear one of us talk about it with one of our government hosts. This road leads northward, to the town of Gramales. To the left, the Bosch mine, to the right thru a local road, Pena Bianca. From here on there is access to a road that leads north of the Matahambre mines and to the port of Santa Lucia where copper taken from the Matahambre mine and the Mora Donkey mines was exported. Here, a Mexican consortium used to extract gold, but now all the mines are closed. If one takes this road South at Pons, it leads to the town of Cabezas located at kilometer 27 of the road of Pinar to Guane. That is to say, about 10 miles before the town of Sumidero. As you may all understand, these are our main escape routes to the north, east and west. There is a road in the town of Guane, the South road, which leads to the city of Pinar Del Rio and from there to the province of Havana. There is also a railway to Havana. At the north point, there is a westward road that leads to Guane and eastward leads to Port Esperanza, the Mulata, Honda Bay, the Bay of Mariel continuing to the city of Havana. We don't know what the condition of the stretch of Santa Lucia to Honda Bay is, but it should be transitable.

I changed the slide.

— Going back to the road of Pinar del Rio to Guane. Leaving the city, there is an old hospital that was used for those with tuberculosis. I have no idea if it is still there. Nearing the town of Cabezas, we pass the Isabel Maria Valley. Here is where the Great Cavern of Saint Thomas is at, the largest one in Cuba as of now. This is also restricted since it has been militarized but it is not top secret. – I continue – This cavern was initially used during the cold war. It was used to station Russian missiles. There is even a mechanism within it that slides the roof in the event that a missile is fired. I had the opportunity to visit the cavern once the missiles were uninstalled and I saw the concrete and zinc ceiling they had built. They were also stationing refueling tanks. The interesting part is that all operations were under the order of Lieutenant Angel Hernandez Rojo, an ex official of the General Batista regime, the same regime Castro overthrew. Rojo asked and was granted asylum in the Brazilian embassy in Cuba. By this I mean, he didn't finish the job.

I explained all of this just as a historical footnote. Everyone was paying close attention to what I was saying. I then continued with the details of our plan:

- Just after the town of Sumidero, there is a village with 5 or 6 little houses near a road next to a residual hillock where the Herreria Cavern is located and can be seen from the road. The mounting range that goes thru the town of Sumidero to the town of Calientes has various brooks one of which forms the Amistad Cavern discovered in 1961 by a Polish-Cuban expedition sponsored by the then called Cuban Academy of Science that explored 100 caverns from Oriente to Pinar del Rio. My informants have told me that there was an explosion within it where two young locals died. This leads me to believe that they might have been building a military road. Once out of the Village of Calientes, we are out of, but still near military zones. From there we will go north through local roads passing through an isolated hillock located in the Luis Lazo Valley called El Junco. I remember that in this same hillock there is a small but peculiar cavern named the Marrero Cavern.

I looked at all of them and noticed they were taking notes. I didn't want to give so much information that they couldn't retain in their minds. I continued:

- We will keep northbound until we reach the Sierra de los Organos mountain range where we will camp near El Palmar brook, Fuentes Creek, part of the Mesa mountain range. Here we will have reached our objective, The Fuentes Cavern.

Everyone was getting more enthusiastic about the mission. I thought this was the perfect time to explain why it was so important that we reach our objective:

— Let me tell you about the Fuentes Cavern – I said – It was discovered in October of 1961, during a Polish-Cuban expedition. The ones involved were: The Wysokogórski Polish Club, the Scientific Exploration Club and members of the Speleology Department of Cuban Academy of Science.

As I was explaining to them, my mind wandered back to that very special expedition. I remembered the first ones there were Wieslaw Maczeck, Przemyslaw Burchard, Manuel Acevedo, Fernando Jiménez and me.

I had been a part of many expeditions up until 1967. We had done approximately 5 or 6 miles of cartographic material, obtaining the largest longitudes inside one same gallery. This was the largest riverbed discovered in Cuba.

A few years afterwards, I learned that they had continued expeditions at various levels and that the distances had grown.

I then realized that I was probably giving these guys information that they did not need. So I decided to, once and for all, relate one of the most unusual anecdotes of my life.

— Let me tell you about something that happened during one of our visits. – I said – We were in a Group of four: Andy, Glenn, Feito and I. We were walking through the Pica Pica mountain range. I remember we were carrying enormous backpacks and it was getting late. We went in through the Palmar river into the cavern and we found a small opening that leads to an area where we could camp out for the night. We fell asleep almost immediately, listening to the sound of the river, the birds and insects that were close by.

I could tell the guys were growing anxious with my story, so I continued;

— I do not know how much time passed but I was awakened by an intense red light that came through one of the openings of the cavern. I called Andy, who was next to me and, as he woke up, the light changed from red to an even brighter white that disappeared after a few seconds. We woke Glenn up and the white, bright light appeared again. We could not wake up Feito but the most interesting part about what was happening was the sudden silence. We could not hear the sound of the river nor of the insects or animals. It was an eerie silence. We didn't move for hours and eventually fell asleep. The next morning we went outside but couldn't see anything strange. We couldn't hear the sound of helicopters, there were no beings for miles around us and the walls of the mountain were not safe to walk due to vertical position. Now, 40 years later, we have all seen movies that make reference to a bright White Light that comes from extraterrestrial beings. Was that what happened that night? We never found out.

Norman interrupted:

— I am growing more and more interested in this place. Please go on.

— I know you will be as intrigued as I have been for so many years. – I said and continued my story – A few months went by and we were exploring a higher side of the mountain range in search of other levels of the cavern. We got to a hill and I had the radiation detector that you – looping at Norman – had prepared for us. Right at that moment, the alarm came on. It was the first time I had heard it since we tried it out at the University of Havana. We marked the place and continued our exploration of the area. We never found any other radioactive signals, so we thought maybe it had been a meteorite. A few years later, we found radiation inside one of the galleries inside the cavern but we still didn't know where it was coming from. Then one day, I found something – My eyes rolled thinking back to that moment in my youth – Then I couldn't continue my explorations of the zone. Work and politics got in the way and I had to leave Cuba. That was 27 years ago.

Norman and John were now even more intrigued. They both asked at the same time:

- But what did you find?

- It was something made out of some kind of metal but it was almost completely buried under the Rocks. Now do you realize why we need explosives?

Norman kept talking to himself. He couldn't believe the story and kept looping at me:

- How have you been able to keep this secret for so many years?

- I couldn't do anything else. I didn't have any means or contacts to help me do what we plan to do now.

John interrupts us:

- Well, now that I know the story, I think I am going to make some other calls to see if we can get some more help in the event we need it. This is getting to be more complex by the minute.

I Looked at the guys and said:

- I hope you are now much more interested in our trip!

All of them agreed. We talked for a while Langer and then it was time for them to leave.

- We will not see each other until we are in Cuba. Good luck to all.

THE SENDOFF

JULY 20TH

IT WAS MY LAST DAY AT WORK. I WAS HAVING LUNCH WITH SOME other doctors at Palm Springs Hospital in Hialeah. We were talking about usual topics such as the stock market, baseball and politics. I'm telling them I was leaving on vacation and one anesthesiologist says.

— Vacation again? You just came back from the Dominican Republic!

Some neurologist starts cracking jokes about me going away to a fat farm to lose some weight. The cardiologist asks:

— Are you going on a safari?

The eldest of the group, a retired doctor says:

— Rambo is going hunting!

— I'm going on some explorations. When I get back, I'll tell you all about it. – I said.

Through the hallways, I bumped into some other surgeons and X-ray technicians. While wishing me well, they ask me to bring back a hunting trophy.

I passed by the doctors lounge to have some Cuban coffee prepared by Panchito and said goodbye to some other doctors. I felt somewhat sad. I had a feeling I wasn't coming back.

I was on my way out when I bumped into another neurologist. I said goodbye to him and opened the door to the parking lot. I took a couple of steps and turned back to give the hospital building another look. See you soon! -I said to myself.

I drove to my office just to leave everything in place. I had no patients scheduled. I left all the numbers of the doctors that would be covering for me and picked up some medical supplies we might have a need for.

THE TRIP

JULY 20TH

EARLY IN THE MORNING NORMAN, MIRIAM AND I ARE AT THE MIAMI International Airport. We have a lot of baggage and as it was to be expected, we are delayed. They look through the baggage and ask us what the reason for our trip to Cuba is. I show them the State Department's permission to travel as a scientific mission. Finally, after two hours we crossed the departure gates. The plane is also delayed, something not at all unusual, and after another two hours we are asked to board. Cubans traveling to the island to visit their families surround us. I tell Miriam and Norman that if anyone asks, we too are traveling to visit family members. We finally take off. Miriam is deathly afraid of the take off and of.... the landing. After a few minutes they told us that we are about to touch down at the Jose Marti airport in the city of Havana.

After touchdown, we walked down the boarding stairs towards the terminal building. The building was surrounded by military dressed in army greens. I crunched at the site. Once inside the terminal building we stood in line but a government official came over towards us and took us to a lateral door. As soon as he opened the door the first thing I saw was Andy. He came towards me and greeted us enthusiastically. The expression on the other official's faces changed from frowns to smiles. They walked us through Customs without a hitch. Outside there were Russian jeeps with drivers who took care of the luggage.

Andy said:

- The rest of the heavy baggage will be picked up by them on a truck. I mean all the speleology equipment that we will, generously, donate to the state once we are finished.

It was obvious that this "arrangement" had been made with the government previously and it made them very happy since among all the equipment we also had boots, uniforms, personal items, canned foods etc. We left towards Havana. After a short while, we reached the Riviera Hotel in the Vedado section. Miriam got teary eyed. We were just two blocks away from what had been our home. Many memories came to mind, us strolling through the Malecon with our then little girls. Carefree days of hope and daydreaming! We reached the hotel's entrance and Andy walked with us to the front desk. Without saying a word, they knew who we were. They greeted us graciously, handed us the keys to our two double rooms and the bellhops took care of the luggage.

Andy told us he would be picking us up around 7:30 PM for dinner at Tropicana.

- Good! Let's start sightseeing! – I said as he walked out.

Miriam and Norman had been instructed not to say anything compromising inside the rooms since they were surely tapped and had cameras monitoring us. This was something that many agents that had deserted the government had assured us of. After taking a shower and resting a little, we went down to the hotel bar. Miriam had a Daiquiri and Norman and I ordered Cuba Libres. After chatting for a while, I told them:

- Let's stroll through the Malecon!

I said it loud enough for some of the employees to hear us, some of whom were surely instructed to spy on us. We crossed the street. It was early, around 4 o'clock and there was a blazing sun, the reason why there were not many people strolling around. I took the opportunity, took out a small cellular phone and an earpiece, and very discreetly placed the earpiece in my right ear with my head turned towards the sea. I called Tony in Lawton. I told him to contact "his friend" and tell him to be at his house tomorrow at 6 AM. That we would be there around 7 or 8. I asked him to tell Tony to be discreet, not to let anyone see this person enter his house and to tell him to bring me the information.

I took off the earpiece and put it away along with the cell phone and we kept on walking.

We returned to the hotel's bar and asked for another round of drinks. The bartender said:

— You came back very quickly.

— Yes – I answered. It's too hot, too much sun.

Andy showed up at 7:30 sharp to pick us up. This time he had a small tourism van with a driver. We got in and left towards Marianao passing through the 5th Avenue tunnel.

— It's been a long time since I've been here. I think I've forgotten the streets! – I said.

We had a hearty meal and enjoyed a great show at Tropicana. Miriam and I even danced a little. We left Tropicana late, around 1 AM. When we got back to the Riviera Hotel Andy asked:

— What would you like to do tomorrow?

— I don't know, we are very tired. We are going to be getting up around nine so call me around that time and we'll decide then. – I answered.

> – It's a deal - Andy said, and left.

Miriam asked me:

> – Why didn't you tell him what we want to do tomorrow?

> – It's not convenient here to let anyone know a day ahead what your plans are. – I answered.

We took the elevator to our rooms. We looked out the window at the tranquil sea covered by the moonlight.

> – Well I guess it's time to sleep. We have many things to do tomorrow. – I said.

JULY 21ST

Norman woke us up with a knock at the door. It was 9 AM.

> – Get up sleepy heads. It's time for breakfast! – He said through the door.

> – Yes, wait for us downstairs. – I answered – We'll be there in a few minutes.

As said, a few minutes later we were downstairs. We found him at the hotel restaurant. Norman was already gulping down his breakfast.

> – I see you woke up with an appetite this morning. – I said.

> – Yes, it was all that drinking last night. – He answered.

We were halfway through breakfast when Andy arrived.

> – Hello. How are we all doing? – He asked.

- Hungry after all the drinking last night. – I answered. Sit down and have breakfast with us.

Andy sat next to me, called the waiter and ordered his breakfast. We started chatting and he asked:

- What have you planned for today?

- We want to get to the central part of Havana. We could have lunch at the Bodeguita del Medio and then walk it off towards the Cathedral Plaza. We can take some pictures there and Miriam can do some shopping. I guess after that we can go to Lawton so Miriam can see her family and give them the presents she brought for them. Tonight we can have dinner at the hotel. – I answered.

- Sounds great to me – He answered – Let me call the Driver to bring the van. We'll be off in a half hour.

- Great! – I said.

Everything is working out just right, I thought to myself. The van is probably outside already and they are making a call to inform someone about our unplanned trip to Lawton.

Half an hour later, the three of us went to the hotel lobby. Andy was already waiting for us there.

- Are we ready?

- Yes – We answered and followed him outside where the same small van with the same driver was waiting for us.

We drove off passing by the Malecon and the American Embassy, which was heavily guarded by government police, and by dozens of flagstaffs with makeshift flags, the Cuban government had positioned in front it to obstruct its view. We made no comments. We kept on going towards the Punta castle. We could see the deterioration of the buildings, the lack of paint, and the lack of maintenance. Most were in ruins. We took a turn and went up Prado Street. Everything looked the same as it did years ago. We reached Central Park and saw all the old buildings that surround it and beyond the Capitol. We passed by the Havana Institute and made a turn towards Havana's port. Here, the destruction was evident. It looked like a city that had been bombed. Finally, we reached the Cathedral plaza. We went into a bar and asked for some beers. It was a very hot day. Miriam decided to go buy some knick-knacks being sold to tourists while we stayed talking and enjoying our cold beer taking cover of the blazing sun under some umbrellas.

While sitting under the umbrella, I saw Miriam being "escorted" by our driver. When they returned, I asked the driver if he would like something to drink and he said yes. Miriam was feeling the hot sun, so she ordered a cold beer. After we finished our beers, we went over to the front of the Cathedral and took some pictures. We had been walking for two hours and I said to Andy:

— It's almost one o'clock. I think it's about time for lunch.

We walked a bit more towards the Bodeguita del Medio.

Andy went ahead of us, entered the restaurant, and whispered something in the ear of one of the waiters who in turn spoke to another waiter and told him to accommodate us. It's a small restaurant. They sat us at a corner table for five.

— You know, this is the first time I set foot in this place. – I said looking around - Even though it was already famous when I was a young person, I never came here.

Andy started telling me the history of the place and we ordered lunch. We spent two pleasant hours listening to traditional Cuban music played by a guitar trio and after a couple of beers I paid the check and turned to Andy:

- Let's get back to the hotel. Miriam needs to do some things and I want to show you something.

- OK – Andy said.

We left Bodeguita towards the van. We got in and drove off towards the Riviera Hotel. When we got there we told Andy we would be ready in half an hour and went up to our rooms. After refreshing ourselves and putting on some fresh clothes, Miriam got all the things she had brought for her family as gifts and I got a gift I had ready for Andy. I called Norman and told him we were going to go visit Miriam's family. I told him to "be good" and to wait for us at the Hotel. We took the elevator down to the lobby and there was Andy and the driver waiting for us.

- We're ready – I said.

We followed them towards the van and just as I was seating in the seat directly behind the driver I leaned forward and whispered to Andy:

- This is a gift for you. Keep it in a safe place.

We gave the driver the address: Armas street in Lawton and started our way.

We went up Paseo Street in El Vedado. Passed by The Revolution Plaza, the Marti monument. Turned on Rancho Boyeros Avenue up to The Rotonda in front of the Clinico Quirurgico Hospital where I worked many years ago, and up to Lacret street in the city of La Vibora.

From there we kept northwards towards Dolores avenue in the city of Lawton. We stayed on Armas street, turned right and parked in front of Miriam's family home. We got out of the car and I asked Angel to come with us. We knocked at the door and Miriam's sister opened it. Between tears of joy and hugs, she called for husband to come to the door and everyone wrapped themselves in a group hug.

I turned around and said to Angel:

- I think it will be best for you to leave and pick us up in a couple of hours. We'll have dinner at the hotel.

- I understand – He answered. – It's a family reunion. They've been many years apart.

He said goodbye to everyone and left.

Once I made sure they had left I quietly asked Tony:

- Do you have the package?

- Of course I do. Come with me. Let's leave the girls alone, they have a lot to talk about.

We walked through the hallways of the old cement house with its timber and tile roof.

- It's incredible the way you have kept up the place. – I said.

- Believe me it hasn't been easy. – He answered.

We walked through the kitchen and reached the back room. Inside I found an old, extremely thin white haired man.

- Are you Pepe? – I asked

He nodded his head and asked:

— Are you Pastor?

— Yes, I am – I answered.

I turned to Tony and asked him:

— Please leave us alone. Go back, see what the girls are up to, and if they come this way, let me know.

— OK – He answered and left.

Once alone, we sat down and I asked him to tell me what his friend Pedro in Miami said he knew.

— I really don't know what it's all about. I'm just doing a friend a favor. He has helped me out of many problems I've had with the government. He even got a doctor to certify that I was insane so they would let me free. I was in prison just for being against the government. – He answered.

— How did you become a friend of his? – I asked.

— Slowly. We did favors for each other. He didn't have many friends. He didn't talk much, just to his wife and his daughter. I don't think he has any other family. Once, while I was over at his house fixing a range, there was a knock at the door. I kept quiet in the kitchen because I didn't want anyone to know I knew him. He opened the door and there was a government representative with a package for him from another high government official. They sat in the living room talking about different subjects. Lazaro, my friend, asked the other guy if he wanted a drink and got up and got a bottle of rum. They drank and then they touched on a subject that caught my attention. They started talking about the Spanish government granting Spanish citizenship to descendants of Spaniards. That meant that the children of the top ranking government officials, primarily those of Fidel and Raul could obtain a Spanish passport, guaranteed. – He continued telling me the story - And that he, the other guy, thought to do the same since he knew of other government officials who were doing it assuring themselves of a way out in case of any political turmoil in the island. After the government official left, Lazaro returned to the kitchen. He looked lost in his thoughts. I asked him:

— What worries you?

— I have no Spanish blood in me. I have no way out. - He answered.

I placed my arm over his shoulder and told him that there was always a way out and that I would help him find it. Some time after that, he called and said he had found a way out but that he needed my help finding a contact in YUMA (Cuban slang for USA). I asked what type of contact he needed in the USA and he said he needed to contact someone in the US government. I told him that would be difficult to do but that I would try. We didn't touch the subject again.

— When and where can I talk to him? – I asked – I have only 48 hours left. We're leaving on a trip in three days.

- I will contact him early tomorrow. – He answered.

- Good. Give him my name. Tell him to contact me at The Riviera Hotel in El Vedado. You can tell him that we met many years ago at the Calixto Garcia Hospital where I worked. That I treated a family member of yours or a friend. Describe me to him so he will recognize me. Tell him to wear his uniform. By the way, What is his name? – I asked.

- Lieutenant Colonel Lazaro – He answered.

- You tell him I will be having lunch at 12 noon and dinner at seven for the next two days. Tell him everything has been arranged. You are not to speak to anyone about this.

Putting my hand in my pocket, I got out four one hundred dollar bills and told him:

- There will be more where this came from if everything turns out all right. By the way, what does he look like?

- He is shorter than you. Tanned, black curly hair, very dark brown eyes and has the accent of those native to the western side of the island. He walk limping with his right foot, sequel to an injury in the angolan war.

- Ok, thanks for all the information. Stay here. I'll have Tony bring you some food. Don't leave until nighttime and take a different route home just in case someone is following you.

I shook his hand as a way of saying goodbye. Closed the door behind me and went back to the living room. We kept on talking with Miriam's family for a couple of hours and after a teary goodbye went on our way back to the hotel. We went directly to the hotel restaurant where the waiters immediately took our order and I called Norman's room.

- Hello! – He answered – I'm starving. It's about time you got back.

- Well get yourself to the restaurant, we've already ordered! – I said.

We had a wonderful dinner and after the mandatory coffee, Andy asked:

—   So, what are your plans?

—   As you know, we need to wait for the others that will be
    joining us in the expedition. They are supposed to get here on
    the 24th in the morning. I hope you can find out at what time
    they will be arriving so we don't have to spend the whole day
    at the airport. – I said – Tomorrow we plan to stay at the hotel
    to enjoy the pool and just relax. If you have any information
    about the time of their arrival, call me so we can plan our day.

—   OK – Andy said as he shook my hand and said good-bye. –
    Thanks for the gift. Too much for me – He added.

—   You deserve it! – I answered.

As soon as Andy left, we walked out to the pool area and sat down.
We could see the moon's reflection on the water. The breeze was
calming and we just chatted for a while. Norman turned to Miriam
and asked:

—   So how did it go with your family?

Miriam got emotional and answered:

—   You cannot imagine. I had not seen them for 27 years!

I changed the conversation and told Norman:

—   I'm very happy.

Norman smiled. He already knew about my meeting.

After enjoying the surroundings for a while, we opted to go up to our
rooms so we could sleep. Tomorrow was going to be an exciting day.

JULY 23RD

We woke up early and after breakfast, we put on our bathing suits and walked out to the pool.

We swam for a while and laid down to get some sun under such a beautiful tropical sky. Miriam asked for a piña colada and I opted for a Margarita. Norman preferred a beer.

It was close to 11 by the time we went up to the room to shower and come back for lunch.

It was exactly noon and we were sitting at the restaurant ordering lunch. We were in no hurry as we were waiting for someone to come by but nobody was showing up.

Just as we were saying that, Andy arrived:

 - Hi! How is everything?

 - You arrive at the perfect time – I said – Sit down and have lunch with us.

He sat down and I called for the waiter who was close by. We ordered and the food came right away. As we were enjoying our lunch, Andy said:

 - I inquired about the flight and they confirmed they are getting here tomorrow at 3 PM. They need to wait for a flight from Japan where some diplomats are traveling.

 - Good! – I said – We can leave here at two.

We had some Cuban coffee and said goodbye until the next day. I was not very happy, as the interview had failed. We needed to wait until later that afternoon.

We spent the whole afternoon in our rooms, relaxing and reading some magazines.

At around 6:30 I was so hungry I wanted to go down to the restaurant. Miriam made me wait until seven at which time we stopped by Norman's room to pick him up and went straight to the restaurant.

As we walked in, I heard a voice:

  – Pastor! How nice to see you! – He said

I saw someone coming towards me. He was dressed in uniform and had a problem with his right leg. He extended his hand out to me.

  – Lazaro! I am so happy to see you! – I said as I realized who it was. – Please, have dinner with us!

I could see the smiles on the employees' faces as we walked towards our table.

After ordering and enjoying our dinner, I said:

  – Did Pepe explain?

He answered by nodding his head as he practically whispered:

  – I brought you half. The other half over there (in the US). It is him, his wife and their 5-year-old daughter.

He passed an envelope under the table. I grabbed it and immediately attempted to hide it.

  – Pepe will let you know what you have to do – I said – Just give us a couple of days.

We never touched the subject again. We just continued talking about the good old times, when I took care of his family at the Calixto Garcia hospital. This last part I try to say loudly so that the security around us could hear.

After coffee, we said goodbye with a good handshake.

We went up to our rooms. Miriam held my hand. She could tell I was nervous but we could not speak about anything.

We went to bed early. Tomorrow we had to work: The rest of the team was arriving.

Once our lights were off, I hid the sealed envelope in my Money belt, just to make sure that I had it with me at all times.

I tried to sleep but I couldn't. I kept wondering what was inside the envelope. Could it be true? Could it be a plan just to arrest us? With all these thoughts in my head, I could only sleep a few minutes at a time.

THE TEAM ARRIVES

THE SUN COMES UP. MIRIAM LOOKS AT ME AND SAYS:

- It is obvious that you did not sleep well.

- I couldn't. – I said – I have too many things to worry about.

We got dressed and went down to the restaurant for breakfast. We then went back up to our rooms. The morning dragged by until noontime, when we went back to the restaurant for lunch. We were sitting at our table when Andy arrived.

- I have news – he said – There is a possibility that the flight may be coming in ahead of time.

- OK – I said – We are ready. Do you think we have time for lunch?

- Yes – he answered – but then we need to leave.

We told the waiter to bring lunch for Andy and me in a hurry, as we had to leave. Norman and Miriam would stay behind at the hotel.

We had a quick lunch, said goodbye to Miriam and Norman and left with Andy on our way to the Jose Marti airport in Havana.

It took us about a half an hour to get there. The driver stopped at the front entrance and Andy and I stepped into the building on our way to the Terminal area. Once there, Andy spoke to one of the airport officials and he informed him that the flight had just arrived. Andy turned to me and said:

    — I am going to see if I can expedite the immigration process. Wait for me here.

I sat down in one of the few available chairs and waited for Andy to get back.

It was about an hour later when the door to the gate opened and Andy walked out. John, Bill, Tommy, Ben and Hans followed him.

Even though John speaks Spanish, he greets me in English. The rest of the guys do the same.

    — How was your trip? – I asked John.

    — OK. I've had better. – He answered.

We stepped out of the airport and the driver was waiting for us. There was another small vehicle next to ours that would fit the rest of the passengers.

I introduced John to Andy as well as the rest of the guys. We got into the vehicles and went on our way back to the Riviera Hotel.

As soon as we got to the hotel Andy approached the front desk. He had reserved three double rooms for the rest of our group.

Everyone went up to their respective rooms to take a shower and relax. We agreed to meet in the restaurant at 7:00 PM.

That night we had agreed to meet with Andy so that we could plan when we could start off for Fuentes.

There is a lot of expectation to see if Fidel Castro will attend the celebrations of the 26th of July, which is the date the government commemorates the Assault of the Moncada in Santiago de Cuba. His health is something that worries everyone here. We will probably not be able to leave until the 27th, but that is only tentative. We'll see what happens tonight.

At exactly 7:00 PM, we all meet in the restaurant. The guys are really hungry after a whole day without food.

The personnel at the restaurant have reserved a long table for us as our group is now made up of 10 people on our side and 2 or 3 more on the Cuban side.

Andy came in a little later with two guests. He approached me and introduced one of the guys who seemed to be about 20 years old:

– Carlos is in charge of the Speleological department in the zone that you want to visit and Luis is his assistant. When I am not available, they will take care of getting you all the necessary supplies and answer any questions you may have. – He said.

We sat down to dinner, everyone asked according to their own individual taste. The Americans practically ordered a whole cow for themselves!

During dinner, the conversation turned to the celebrations of the 26th of July. They told us that because of the celebration and for security reasons, we could not go on our trip until the 27th at 9:00 AM. We would have a bus pick us up and a truck would follow us with all the cargo and supplies.

We would go directly to the Caliente town where three Russian jeeps would be waiting for us. These jeeps, and their individual drivers would be with us all the time at the campsite. The three jeeps and the truck would get us as close to the mountain range as possible. From there we would walk to the Rio Las Palmas where we would camp.

After going over every detail, we said goodbye until July 27th.

John told me we now had 2 days to rest and relax at our leisure.

—   OK! – I said – Let's get some rest. We will talk tomorrow.

JULY 25TH

I get up very early just to pace up and down the room. I can't wait until it is 8:00 AM, as this is the time we said we would go down to the restaurant for breakfast.

Miriam gets up and looks at me wondering what I am doing up so early. She knows I am no early riser.

—   Come on, get dressed so we can go down for breakfast. – I said.

—   What's the hurry? – She answers – It's only 7:30 AM.

We finally went downstairs. We are the first ones to sit down. A few minutes later John walks in and sits next to me. The rest of the group starts arriving one by one. I turn to John.

—   After breakfast we need to talk.

—   OK – John says.

We finish breakfast and tell the guys they have the day off to enjoy the pool.

Miriam, John and I get up and walk to the Hotel's main entrance. As we are going down the stairs, a young man approaches us and asks if we need a taxi. I tell him we don't as we plan to walk on the Malecon.

We cross the street and walk towards the Almendares river. This is the most deserted area. I get on the phone and call Tony.

- Hello?

- Tell Pepe that we cannot talk until the 29th or the 30th – I say and rapidly hang up the phone.

- What is wrong? – John asks.

- I have many things to tell you. The first one is that, on the 23rd, I met with the main guy and he gave me part of the information.

- So what does it say? – John asks.

- I don't know. It is in a sealed envelope and I wouldn't dare open it here. There are too many eyes and ears on us. What I also have to tell you is that I told him I would get back to him in a couple of days but that is not going to be possible, – I continue – as you first have to coordinate with your friends (CIA), so they can pick up the main guy with two family members. You will have to do this once we are out there in the campground.

- As soon as you have all the details as to where they have to be picked up, we will send the information – John says – What about the envelope? Where is it?

- We will see it in the cavern or somewhere out there where it's safe.

We walked back to the Hotel with no problem. We had only gone as far as a couple of blocks so nobody was suspicious.

Before we got to the Hotel, I told John I was wondering if Fidel was going to make an appearance the next day.

- He is too old and sick, but nothing would surprise me. – I said.

We had lunch later on around the pool and spent the rest of the day relaxing, swimming and chatting about sports. We got a couple of hours' sleep on the reclining chairs on the poolside.

It was late so we went up to shower and then came down again for dinner.

After that, we said goodnight to the guys and each one of us went back up to their respective rooms.

JULY 26TH

It was early in the morning when we woke up and turned on the television set. Everything seemed quiet and the only comments on TV were with reference to the celebration of this official day for the Cuban Revolution.

We went down to the pool and stayed away from any political subjects in our conversation. We never spoke about the Commandant's health either.

At the end of the day we found out that Fidel had not been present in the Celebration acts and that Raul Castro said they were still in the "periodo especial" or special period as they call it, which means they will be reducing the food rations and there will only be more hunger for the people. He also said the Commandant's health is still grave.

We went to sleep early, as we knew they would be picking us up the next day at 9:00 AM.

JULY 27TH

It is raining as we wake up. Our bags are ready and we go down for breakfast.

At about 9:30 AM, Andy arrives, explaining he is late because of the rain.

— We are ready! – I say as we walk towards the front desk and ask the bellman to bring down our bags.

The bus was parked right at the entrance and the bellhops were putting our bags in the back. Once everything is ready, they ask us to board. Miriam and I take the first seat on the right hand side while Andy sits behind the driver next to another young guy. The rest of our group just took whatever other seats they wanted.

We were very comfortable. The bus had about 30 seats and there were only eight of us, plus two Cuban residents.

It was 10:00 AM by the time the bus began the journey to Pinar del Rio. We went up Paseo Boulevard, we were able to see what was left of the house where we used to live. As we approached Linea Street, the driver made a right turn on our way to the tunnel. From there we drove through Marianao, and going down the hill we saw what was left of the old building where the Exploration Group's office used to be, as we continued on thru the Central Highway to Pinar del Rio.

As we went thru Herradura, I turned to Andy:

- Do you remember the Rancho Mundito Cavern?

- Yes! – He answered and smiled.

That particular cave used to be a subterranean river and now it is where their leader has one of his summer homes.

We drove on and, approximately four hours later we finally reached Ciudad de Pinar del Río. I barely recognize it in the horrible condition it is in.

We stopped at a tourist's area, but I don't remember the name. We had lunch but not as good as the one at the Hotel.

After lunch, we got back on the bus and went on our way.

We were now on Guane highway, which is not very wide and extremely dangerous. It has a few very old iron bridges and it is only a One Way. The tight curves through the mountains made us very uneasy.

We went through the Cities of Cabezas and Isabel Maria and finally got to the small town of Sumidero. We stopped in front of the park and noticed a large truck and three Russian jeeps that were parked there.

- We're here – Andy said – We need to change vehicles.

We got out and walked over to the jeeps. The drivers were already getting our bags and backpacks out of the bus. Miriam, Andy and I got into the first jeep. The rest of the group divided themselves amongst the other two.

Once we were all in the jeeps, Andy took charge and all the vehicles started on their way to Guane. We went by a small town of Caliente and further up turned right to get on a side street in very poor condition.

The jeeps were jumping up and down from the potholes. It was good that there was no rain.

We could hear the truck that was following us. The driver was having an even harder time in this damaged and run down street. We finally got to a small valley, quite plain right next to a river and close to the mountains.

   – Right here! – Andy said.

The jeeps stopped and we all got out stretching our legs.

Andy asked the drivers to unload as fast as they could, as he didn't want nightfall to catch us halfway of getting everything ready. The drivers hurried up as did the driver of the truck who started unloading the boxes.

Our guys ran out to get the boxes where the tents were and before we realized it, they had already built four of them on the North side of the valley. Each tent was big enough for two people. They started to bring in their bags and backpacks as well as ours.

They then built a much larger tent that would serve as the main tent where we could eat and where we could meet.

They then finished building the other four tents on the South side. These would be assigned to the Cuban residents that were assigned to us.

The last tent that was built was the one that would hold the food and all the supplies that by now were sitting in the middle of nowhere.

Andy was pleasantly surprised at how fast the guys had been able to put up all the tents. I told them they were used to doing this in much worse places with snow, rain and a lot of wind.

Before night started to fall, everything was built including the lights for each tent and area. We even had a small emergency generator.

I approached John and told him what a great job he and the guys had done. I also mentioned the great idea of placing our tents on one side and the tent for our "close friends" on the other side so that we could have some privacy. I was delighted.

Among the new Cuban residents now with us was Cheo. He was going to be our cook and would stay at the campsite all the time.

Andy also introduced me to another Speleologist knowledgeable of the zone. His name was Malagon.

The guys opened some of the boxes that carried supplies and started to distribute them to all. We had spam, chocolate, etc.

- Not bad for today – Andy said – By tomorrow, we will have hot food as Cheo is getting the kitchen ready. All of the kitchen and the pots and pans were on the last jeep. They also had some ice chests, meat, etc.

It started to rain and we went under the main tent. Andy told us that we would be having a large breakfast the next day so we could start off to the cavern. He mentioned we would be getting back late.

- We are going to explore the first level, so we will have to take some rafts in order to cross the river – Andy said – the river is approximately 500 ft. and it lies on the right side of the cavern. That part has never been explored so we don't know where the spring water comes from. We will then continue to the dry side while we can because if it starts to rain hard, then the water will create a problem with the small river that lies inside of the mountains and that only has more water during the rainy season.

We listened as Andy continued explaining:

- Every morning, before we leave, we will make sure to listen to the weather report so that we are not caught in the middle of a flood inside the cavern. That would be very dangerous.

After listening to all the final details, I said to Andy:

- I suggest we go relax now. Tomorrow is going to be a hard day.

Everyone agreed. It was already dark by the time we all went into our own tents. John's tent was right next to mine and I could stick my head inside his. I try to speak very low so nobody can hear us:

- We need Tommy to get in touch with your people and tell them to pick up the three packages at the Cepero Cavern in Camarioca, which is in the Matanzas province on the 31st. They should wait for them for two days.

- OK – John answered.

I got back in my tent and went to bed with thoughts of what tomorrow may bring.

The night breeze came in through the screen that protected us from the insects. I slowly fell asleep.

JULY 28TH

The sun comes up and I wake up to the wonderful smell of fresh coffee. I get up and go down to the river to wash off.

There is a dense fog and I can barely see 100 ft in front. John gets close and tells me that last night the delivery was made. He also said that we would hear more from them by tonight.

As we were going back to the tent, we saw Miriam who was on her way to the river.

- We'll see you at the main tent. – I said and continued walking with John.

We got to the main tent and on top of a large table, Cheo had placed a coffee maker with fresh coffee, milk, sugar and some plates with bacon and eggs. He also had different types of bread and butter. At another table, there was a large container with Orange Juice and ice.

- This is a great breakfast! – I said to Cheo as we sat down to enjoy it.

Miriam finally came in:

- You didn't wait for me! She said,

- Just hurry up or you won't get any! – I said.

After we finished breakfast, we got our backpacks and finally started off on our way to the entrance of the Cavern.

We walked next to the river until we reached some large rocks that seemed to come down from the mountains. They had apparently gotten together to form a wonderful area through many years of avalanches due to heavy rains.

We started to climb the rocks. It was very hard as we had a lot of equipment.

We got to the first level of the Cavern. It was not very large. Actually quite small as compared to the Sumidero on the North side of the hills.

We went by a small opening on the right side and I called Andy:

- – Do you remember?

- – Yes! – Andy said – The light that visited us! – and started laughing.

We continued climbing through the collapsed cave trying to find our way to explore the first level.

Malagon finally yelled out at us. He had found the way.

We reached the spot and there were the marks, with the arrows facing down, that we had painted when we first started exploring the cavern.

We then started walking down the collapsed rocks, we passed all the lights from one to the other as well as the backpacks and the rafts.

We then reached a small beach right next to the river where we used to camp in our many expeditions.

We stopped there and began to inflate the three rafts.

Only two could go on each raft and there were 12 of us. Miriam and I got into one, Carlos – one of the Speleologists – got on another one with Andy and John got on the last one. We each carried a Kerosene lamp, our flashlights, helmets and backpacks.

We navigated through very still waters until we reached the other side. We got off and Carlos went back with the three rafts.

We waited a while and then saw the rest of the group. Carlos with Norman in the first raft. Bill and Ben on the second one and Hans and Luis – the other Cuban resident Speleologist – on the last one. Malagon was swimming behind them.

Once the group was together again, we placed the rafts in a higher area and tied it to a very wide stalagmite so they would not float away in case of a sudden flood.

We walked through the main gallery. In this gigantic area, our reflectors could not even reach how far the longitude was.

- This is incredible. I think I'm on I-95 (comparing the US highway to how wide this area is)

We can see various galleries on each side, both on the main level as well as in the higher level.

Andy tells me that these galleries have never been explored.

I tell him that we should divide into smaller groups.

- You come with Miriam, John and I – Let's explore this gallery to the right. – I say – Norman, Bill and Tommy can go with Malagon through the main gallery so they become familiar with it and Carlos, Ben and Hans can explore the next gallery on the right. I think Luis should stay here so he marks our meeting point.

- I agree – Andy says – We will meet here in eight hours. Does everyone understand?

- Yes! – They all replied.

We got on our way going up on the right side trying to reach one of the galleries that I had always wanted to explore but had been unable to. We were walking quite fast. Miriam and Andy were always a little behind, so I took the opportunity to talk to John:

- This gallery goes East on its way to the Pio Domingo cavern and it leads to a higher level. It would be great if we could find out if there is a connection at all.

- Interesting – John said as we continued to climb up and down the rocks.

We walked for about two hours until we reached an open space with a lake surrounded by beautiful stalactites that simulated a white rock cascade with multicolor lights.

We were quite tired by now, especially since it was the first day and our group was even worse as with John being so young and in such great shape that he walked and walked like there was no tomorrow. We had to stop to take a break!

John told us that if we wanted to relax for a while, he would continue to see if he found anything that was of interest.

- OK! – We gladly replied and John kept on rapidly walking.

- Youth! Nothing like it! – I said to Andy – We are dead tired and he is as fresh as this morning!

- True! – Andy replied smiling.

While we sat there, we started chatting. It was dark and we knew nobody was listening.

He first wanted to express his gratitude for the Rolex watch I had given him. We talked about old times, about old friends, the ones that he has never heard of again, of the ones that have passed on. We simply talked and talked. Then we spoke about the Commandant's health. This is totally forbidden in public.

—   We don't know what will happen if he dies. – He said – But it will never be the same. This will be the end.

We opened some cans of food and sodas and had a marvelous lunch!

Andy looked at his watch and said:

—   We've been here for an hour. I think we need to start walking to see if we meet John.

—   OK – I said as Miriam and I got up and started walking.

We walked for about an hour before we could see the light from John's helmet. He was coming back.

—   So? – I said.

—   Beautiful, there are quite impressive formations that we must take pictures of.

—   We'll see if we have time to come back. There is much more to see – I answered.

—   It is getting late and we need to go back – Andy said – We still have a few hours of walking before we reach the meeting point.

We started our journey back and it took us three hours before we reached the meeting point where the rest of the group was already waiting for us.

Andy told them to start off while we sat down for a few minutes and took a break.

Ten minutes later, Andy got up and told us we needed to get going. We got up and started walking back.

As soon as we got to the riverside on the subterranean river, we saw Luis waiting for us with the three rafts. We got on the rafts and, silently, navigated back.

We climbed up again through the collapsed rocks until we reached the entrance. While everyone was walking towards the campsite, I told Andy we stayed behind so Miriam could take a bath in the river.

- No problem. – He said - That is exactly what I am also going to do down on the other side with the guys. I'll see you both for dinner.

He left and Miriam and I took off our clothes and got in the river.

- How long has it been since we bathed in this river? – I said.

- Too long! – Miriam answered.

We got dressed with clean clothes that we had packed in one of the backpacks we had left at the entrance and walked back to the main campground.

There was a beautiful sunset as we reached the main tent and the smell of food made us even hungrier.

Everyone was sitting at different tables. Cheo, acting as the Chef, would come by with very large pans full of black beans, cassava and in a man-made barbeque pit, there was an enormous pig that looked very appealing.

The guys opened some beer cans and distributed them among everyone as we started devouring this delicious meal.

As soon as we finished, I went over to my tent and came back with four bottles of Guayabita del Pinar (local rum). That made everyone extremely happy.

So the Cuban residents started drinking and drank until late. John approached me and told me that the package would be picked up on the 1st of August at 3:00 AM and, if they encountered any problems, they would repeat the operation the next day.

My heart was beating fast. I had to get some kind of communication tonight!

I said goodbye to all, especially to the Cuban residents who were a little out of it by now. I told Miriam it was time to go to bed.

Once we were inside our tent, I reached for my cell phone. I dialed a number in the US so they could connect me with Tony who was home in Havana.

The telephone rang a couple of times and finally, Tony answered.

- Hello – I said – This is the Reverend. I just wanted to tell you that the church will be sending the prescription packages on July 31st. They will be going to Matanzas province to the house of a church member named Bonifacio who lives after crossing the river to Varadero. Please tell Pepe as soon as you can.

- OK – Tony answered and hung up immediately.

I then called Marta at her house in Florida. She is half-asleep when she answers. I asked her to get paper and pencil.

- Do you have it now? – I ask.

- Yes – She answers.

- Call your father urgently and tell him that a friend of mine will be visiting him with two more people. Have him take him to the farm that same day. Please don't forget.

- OK – She says and hangs up the phone.

I hope she doesn't forget what I say to myself.

All we had to do now was wait. Tired as I was, I fell asleep almost as soon as my head hit the pillow.

JULY 29TH

Dawn is much better today. We awake to the smell of fresh coffee brewing. We continue the same routine of washing our faces in the river and going up to the main store for breakfast. It is there that we all meet to discuss what we did the day before.

After breakfast, we gather our backpacks and go back to the cavern.

We start all over again, trying to to cross over the rumbles and going down to the main area. We travel once more on the rafts and, once we reach the shore, we start to distribute the various chores.

This time it is Andy who wants to go through the second gallery that Carlos, Ben and Hans were able to explore yesterday, finding a lot Ammonite fossils.

Ben & Hans wanted to go with Malagon to explore the main gallery.

I was tired and told them so:

- We are too tired from yesterday so we will stay close to Luis, on the spot that is still the point where we all meet.

The return time for this day was six hours.

Everyone said goodbye and each Group went their own way. After a few minutes I told Luis that we were going to explore a gallery to our left that seemed to be ample enough to walk through.

John, Norman, Miriam and I started walking slowly. We had not even taken more than 40 steps when I asked Norman if he had brought the radioactive detector.

He said yes.

We then started to walk faster.

A few feet forward, we turned right into a gallery and I pointed to an opening in one of the higher spots.

    —   Over there! – I said to John. He immediately went that way and helped us up.

We continued walking, almost running for more than 800 ft. until we came to a cave in.

    —   We're here!!! – I said.

Norman went forward thru the cave in with the radioactive detector on hand and, all of a sudden, all of us could hear the detector sound go on.

Norman stopped it and started to move the rocks with some help from John and me.

A few minutes later, after we were all sweating our hearts out, we could see something metal that was shining through our hand lights.

We looked at our watches. We still had a couple of hours to work, so we continued striving until Norman found what seemed to be a hatchway.

— What do we do now? I asked Norman.

— I don't know, he said. We have to go in but I don't know how.

We don't have much time now. Let's go back and we'll figure out how to solve the problem.

We started back and, so as not to delay, we decided to leave a kerosene lamp and a spare tank.

We finally reached the meeting point. Luis was sleeping with a half-empty bottle of Guayabitas del Pinar still in his hand.

We woke him up and told him to hide the bottle. We didn't want Andy to see it. We started talking to him to get him alert.

After a half an hour, Andy and his group got there with a beautiful sample of Ammonite.

Twenty minutes later, the rest of the Group arrived and we immediately started our way back.

We got to the camping ground much earlier on this day, so I told Andy that I thought it would be better if we took the next day off.

— Remember we also wanted to do some diving – I said.

— It's true. – He said – And relaxing for one day will do wonders for us. I am going to set everything up for tomorrow morning.

Norman told us he would rather stay in to rest. Hans wanted to do the same thing.

>   – Ok. We'll get two jeeps to take us in the morning. – Andy
>   said.

I told John to bring a couple of bottles of rum but to bring the ones that were already "prepared" (to produce diarrhea), so we could give some to the drivers.

Once we had made all the arrangements, we decided to hit the sac. Not before telling Norman that he had all day to go back to the cavern with his group to see if he could get anything done. I also told him that Hans could probably help him by entertaining the onlookers, reminding him that they had to be back by 5 PM at the latest.

>   – Ok. – He said and went to bed.

John told me he was going to send word for the two that were missing and went back to his tent. We could hear the music coming from the large tent. – Good music! – I thought.

It was seven o'clock. I hoped the guys got here with no problem.

JULY 30TH

Dawn came earlier today. Both drivers, Luis and the Speleologist are constantly going to the bathroom.

>   – I think they ate something that didn't agree with them. –
>   Andy says.

>   – Don't worry about it. I took out the first aid kit and gave them
>   a couple of pills to take every four hours.

>   – But they won't be able to drive this way! – Andy said.

— Yes, but don't forget that I have driven these jeeps before and you can drive the other one. I can follow you.

He didn't necessarily like the idea but we were able to convince him. We all left wearing only our bathing suits.

We went by Pueblo del Sumidero and drove North, crossing over Gramales and finally reaching the Santa Lucia port.

We got to the wharf and there was nobody there. Andy parked right in front and I parked under some trees to get some shade. I went to talk to Andy.

Andy said we should go to the town just to let the guards know who we were and what we were planning on doing.

I got in the jeep again and drove to the small station where we found two guys with rifles who signaled us to stop.

Andy gave them his ID and explained that he was part of the expedition.

While this was going on, John had contacted Charles and Jeff, who were hiding in the woods with their backpacks filled with explosives and hiding under some blankets.

We were in the water from 10 until about 1 PM. Just chatting and having some rum – in moderation, of course.

At around 1 PM, we got back in the jeeps and started driving back to Fuentes.

We went by Sumideros and turned right on our way to Caliente. From there we took the neighbors road, until we got close to the camping ground. There, I told Charles and Jeff to jump up so they could hide and we started to sow the way so they could also hide their backpacks.

All of them had specific instructions to cross the river and follow the road to a mountain range about 400 feet from the riverbank. There, they would find a small cave that had a passage to the main gallery, even though the access was not easy.

They would need to crawl about 100 ft with all the equipment before they could get to a place where they could stand. There was a high exit of about 20 ft., where they could camp out, away from all the danger and where they could talk or hear our orders.

We continued on to the camping ground and there everybody was happy to see us. Especially Norman who looked happier than ever. The others had already gotten over their episodes of diarrhea and wanted to thank me for the medication I had given them.

I was talking to everyone while we waited for dinner and I could not hold myself, so I asked Norman:

  –   How is everything?

  –   I'll tell you later, he answered.

We finished dinner and while the guys sat down next to a campfire to chat and have some drinks, I had a chance to go to Norman's tent.

Turns out that John was also there, waiting for me.

Norman started to tell us what had happened in the cavern earlier while we were driving on the coast.

He told us they first went to the river and from there, so that neither the guys, who were busy trying to control their diarrhea and the Cook could see him, he crossed over to the riverbank, entered the cavern and, without giving it a second thought, started running towards the place where we had found the metal.

Once there, he was able to Light the kerosene lamp we had left for him and started to take out all the equipment he had taken.

The first thing he did was test the object to make sure it had electricity and a magnetic force.

Since he thought he was in what seemed to be a hatchway, he took out a special computer, programmed to decipher combinations, codes and languages.

He left the computer on while he explored the surrounding areas.

An hour later, he came back but the computers had not picked up anything.

He sat down and a while later, in the darkness, fell asleep.

He woke up when one of the computers started giving a signal. He got closer to it and was able to see a code with some signs that he could not make out. He saved the data to the computer and pressed enter.

He was surprised when the hatchway opened up and he could observe the interior, shining under a soft violet Light.

Without even thinking about it, he grabbed the computers and went in. Everything around him was metallic. It seemed to be a ship of some kind with metallic walls, soft and bright. There were some signs on the walls and another hatchway to one side.

He looked at his watch, it was already late and he had to get back before anyone noticed he was gone. He took out the computers, turned off the kerosene lamp and, using the additional kerosene we had left for him, he refilled the lamp and started to walk back with the empty container.

John and I couldn't believe it.

—   Then, said John. This is something outside the planet earth. How long has it been since the accident happened?

—   It seems that this happened when the cavern existed.– I said. When it fell over the upper area, it created a landfall, so it is not something that happened millions of years ago. It could have happened anytime, not too many years ago. However, we don't have any knowledge of anything happening during the past few years. No earthquakes, no explosions in the area.

I look at John and I tell him:

—   See if you can get a hold of Charles and Jeff tomorrow and tell them to go through the main gallery and to set up somewhere around the ship. That way they will be able to set up the explosives while Norman looks to see if he can find something else. Make sure you tell them to go out to the entrance of the main gallery every night at midnight so we can get some kind of communication with them.

Turning to Norman I say:

—   Norman, don't forget to take the camera.

—   John I think tomorrow you should go with Norman to the area. We can tell Andy that you are going to stay around the entrance to get some biological species. You guys have less than six hours before we get back.

They were all in accord and we went to sleep.

JULY 31ST

We woke up to the aromatic smell of coffee and as soon as we stepped out of the tents, we could feel a strong wind in our faces. The sky was gray and we could tell a storm was coming.

Andy approached us and told us that the weather report indicated strong storms and that it would be dangerous to go exploring today. He thought it would be better to wait until tomorrow. Supposedly, the storm could mean a couple of days of bad weather.

He told me he had to go to Pinar del Rio and that he would also take the truck so he could get some groceries. He expected to be back tomorrow morning.

I told him not to worry about it and that we would just relax.

After breakfast, Andy left in one of the jeeps and the truck followed him.

We sat down to chat under the tent while we could hear the heavy rain coming down.

John told me this was the moment we had been waiting for. He suggested we diverted the Cubans while he and Norman would just disappear.

Norman and John went back to their tents and the rest of the group stayed chatting in the main tent and decided to play some domino.

A while later Norman and John slipped away through the back of the tents under the heavy rain on their way to the cavern.

All I could think about is that I hoped the cavern would not flood, as it would make it very difficult for them to get out.

John & Norman got to the main gallery and were able to cross over the cave on their way to the side gallery, looking for Charles & Jeff's hiding place. Half an hour later, they finally found the gallery they were looking for.

    — Charles! – John called out.

    — We're here! – Charles answered, turning on the lights on their helmets.

Once they were finally together, John explained that they were changing their station and, with John and Norman helping them with their heavy backpacks, they started walking towards the metal ship.

It took them 45 minutes to get to the area of the cave in, where the ship was.

    — What is that? – Charles & Jeff asked.

    — This is what we came looking for. – John answered, turning over to Norman – I am now leaving with Jeff. We shall meet in the main gallery in four hours. Come back with Charles so that both of them can come back here while we go back to the campground.

    — What are you going to do? – Asked Norman.

    — I am going back to the main gallery and from there we will go up to the higher gallery on the right – the one we explored the first day.

    — What did you find? - Norman asked.

    — Something extremely interesting. – he answered.

– Ok Jeff, just take one of the backpacks with explosives. – John said and they took off immediately.

In the meantime, Norman just kept going back into the ship with even more equipment.

John and Jeff had reached the gallery and, after climbing up with the heavy backpack, they continued at a very fast pace.

– Where is the fire? – Asked Jeff. – Why do we have to rush?

– We still have a long way to go. – Said John. – We can't lose time! The main gallery runs South to North but this gallery runs West to East, through the mountains and it seems that it leads to another cavern that we visited the first day for a few seconds. – He added.

– Today we are going to find out much more than what we saw the first day.

They kept on walking for a couple of hours until John said:

– Hush!

They stood still for a few minutes in total darkness until they could identify the sound of some voices far ahead.

When they couldn't hear the voices any more, they started walking again, turning on their helmet lights occasionally until they could see light coming from underneath.

They took a few steps forward and got to the side of a small opening on the floor.

When they looked down, they couldn't believe their eyes. There was this giant room – probably around four thousand feet at least that is what they could see, as there was a curvature in the walls that made them lose visibility. All of this was clearly illuminated with electricity and in the middle, over gigantic pillars that seemed to be missiles or bombs.

— This seems to be an arsenal. – Jeff seid. – But they don't seem to be conventional weapons. Because of their shape, they remind me of Russian missiles for chemical or bacteriological warfare.

They continued looking and could see a couple of men walking in with a crane and another missile. Both were dressed with yellow uniforms with gloves, boots and their head covered with only a small opening with glass.

— They are bacteriological missiles. – John whispered, as he took out a small camera and took some infrared pictures so they would not be detected. They slowly moved away from the side of the opening.

— Let's position the explosives and prepare the backpack so that after an explosion here, the gallery will cave in and will explode underneath with a delay of a few minutes just to make sure that everything disappears. – John said.

They finished what they had to do and made sure everything stayed hidden before they started their way back. Without the heavy explosives, they could walk faster. They were very tired by the time they reached the main gallery, where they could hear a horrible sound.

The water level had increased about three feet. On the other side were Norman and Charles, who had been waiting for a long time.

— You are finally here! – Said Norman – If we don't hurry, we will not be able to get out!

John and Jeff had a hard time crossing against the current. Charles helped them by throwing them a rope.

John told Charles and Jeff to go back to the ship explaining that he and Norman would try to go back to the campground.

On their way, trying to escape the strong current, they climbed through the collapsed rocks and looked for a way out.

The water continued to climb, making the road even harder. They were both in the water when John finally yelled out to Norman:

- Here! I found the way!

He reached out to Norman who was about to fall over. He pulled him up and placed him on top of a rock.

- Thanks! You saved my life!

- You're welcome. John said. - But let's go now. It is getting really late.

On their way back, John asked:

- So how did it go today?

- Not too well. Said Norman. - It's not easy!

- Was Charles able to place the explosives?

- I think so. - Norman answered.

They finally reached the exit. The river was a turmoil between the water and the sound of the same crashing down. The weather was even worse. It was pouring rain and the lighting seemed to enlighten a gray sky.

After walking through the mud, climbing out of it continuously, they finally reached the campground.

They followed the riverbank and kept falling down until, after quite a few times, they were able to reach their tents.

They were exhausted but they changed and walked over to the main tent.

- Where were you? – I asked.

- Playing with the water. – Norman answered.

Since there were no strangers around, John told me that he had found very interesting things.

- By the way, - I said – Today is the 31st. I wonder if they picked up the packages.

- We'll know tonight, John answered.

- By the way – I said – We need to talk about something that we have forgotten with everything that has been going on. Let's meet at my tent after dinner.

We continued chatting until we sat down to dinner. We had a very typical Cuban meal: White Rice, Picadillo and fried plantains.

After dinner, we had some whiskey to warm us up. Between the humidity and the wind, we were cold.

We left the bottle on top of the table so the Cubans could enjoy it. That would give us some time to talk.

John, Miriam and I went back to my tent. Once inside I told John:

— We have the envelope. Our friend (Teniente Coronel Lazaro) gave it to us, but we have not opened it. I think it is about time we find out, don't you think?

Right at that moment, we heard the jeeps getting closer.

We went out of the tent just as they stopped and we could see a few military men getting out. One of them approached Malagon and greeted him (they looked like they were old friends). Then they started to chat almost in a whisper. They were both gesturing and I could hear Malagon telling him that the entire group was there. The only ones that were not there were Andy and the driver of the truck who had gone to Pinar del Rio.

They continued chatting for a while but seemed to be much calmer. He said goodbye to Malagon, got back in the jeeps and left.

After they had left, Malagon called the rest of the Cubans and they began chatting at one end of the main tent.

We went back to our own tents as the rain was coming down even harder by now.

Once inside my tent, I went to bed. I couldn't help thinking about what those military men had told Malagon.

Thinking and thinking and with the sound of the rain and the river, I finally fell asleep.

AUGUST 1

When we woke up, we could still hear the sound of the rain coming down. We went to the main tent and Cheo had breakfast ready for us.

We had breakfast and chatted for a while. Today was going to be another day gone to waste as the rain was really coming down.

Since I was close to Malagon, I started chatting with him. I asked him how old he was. I told him his last name sounded familiar, etc.

He told me he was born and raised in Pinar del Rio, and that he was still living in the Moncada area in the Isabel Maria valley.

- So you are part of the Malagon family of Isabel Maria! I said. – I think I met your grandfather.

- Really? – He said.

- Yes. That was many years ago, when I was exploring the Santo Tomas cavern.

- And were you able to go inside? (he was probably thinking that it had always been a military zone) Because of his young age, he always knew it as that.

- Yes, I was able to go in many times. First with Nunez Jimenez, when we were looking for some connection among the galleries. After that with Fernando Jimenez, when there were galleries that were used by the military but after that, they took out the missiles.

He listened to me in amazement as he could not understand how a "foreigner" (Cuban exile) could know so much about his land and even know part of his family.

We continued talking for a long time, with anecdotes about the Isabel Maria area (I didn't want to talk too much about the area), but I could not get him to say anything about the military visit.

A while later he told me that today we could not go exploring due to weather conditions. Therefore, I decided to go back to my tent, stopping by John's tent on my way.

I went into John's tent and found him and Norman.

- — Today everything is ruined, as there is no way of going through the water at the entrance. – Norman said.

- — Yes, I know. – I looked at John and asked – What do you think happened for those military men to come in to talk to Malagon?

- — I don't know. – John said. – But I have an idea.

- — What? I said.

He lowered his voice even though it was hard for me to hear him as it was, due to the sound of the rain coming down.

- — We found something in the gallery that lies on the East side of the one we explored the first day.

- — What did you find? – I asked.

- — Well, taking into consideration how long we walked, we assume it is a top gallery that has some kind of access through a small crease on the top to a great cavern, possibly the Pio Domingo Cavern.

- — You must have walked a lot. Possibly more than 2 miles! – I said.

- — Yes, but the important thing is what we saw.

- — So tell me what you saw. – I said.

— Well, it looks like a gigantic deposit of ammunition, but very special ammunition.

— Like what? – I asked.

— Like bacteriological missiles. – John answered.

— So, what does that have to do with the visit of the military men?

— Maybe they have sensors and detected our visit.

— That worries me. I said. We need to take measures to finalize what we have to do.

— I will try to get a hold of the guys. They go out by way of the entrance to the small cave where they go in every night at 12 midnight. – John said.

— By the way, do you know if they picked up the packages? – I asked.

— Yes. Even with the bad weather, they were able to pick up six packages.

— Six? – I asked.

— Yes, it seems there were three more that were not on the list but they pulled it off. The bad weather helped.

— Who were the other three?

— I don't know. John said. We'll know in due time.

Therefore, the day went by with no significant changes. After noon, the weather got better. The rain finally stopped at around 2 but the river was still in turmoil.

After dinner, I asked Malagon if he had heard anything from Andy. He told me they would be arriving the following day, as the road was very bad.

After some conversation, we decided to go to bed.

AUGUST 2ND

We woke up to the noise of motors approaching. We decided to get up and go to the main tent.

We sat down for breakfast and kept hearing the motors trying harder and harder to conquer the mud on the road.

They finally got there at around 9 AM and we saw Andy get out of the jeep and the driver of the truck followed him.

We greeted them and saw the men unloading the truck. They brought boxes of food and a big sack of bread that made everyone very happy.

After that, Malagon called Andy and they went to his tent to talk.

After a few minutes of conversation, they came out smiling and went on to the main tent.

It was there that we all got to talk and Andy told us that the day after would bring us excellent weather so we could go back to the cavern.

It seemed there were no problems or at least he was not giving a second thought to anything.

They also brought some newspapers and magazines for us and the rest of the guys organized a domino game.

We were bored all day but by the afternoon the river had gone down to normal level and the noise of the battling water had given way to a peaceful current.

- Everything looks OK. – I said to John. – We'll see how we can send Norman to his work zone.

- Don't worry about it – John said – He'll be in my group with Bill and Tommy and whatever Cuban they assign. We will send another group out with Ben and Hans and you can take another group with Miriam and possibly Andy.

- By the way – John continued – We already spoke to the guys last night and they finished their work. They also found a small gallery that brought them out to the top of the mountains and they also prepared the explosives there before leaving.

We were able to fall asleep much earlier and were very optimistic.

AUGUST 3RD

It was dawn when as usual, we woke up to the smell of freshly brewed coffee. After breakfast, Andy told us it was time to start walking towards the entrance.

We got our backpacks and walked towards the bank of the river, which led us to the entrance of the Fuentes Cavern. We went up the collapsed rocks and got to the main level. We continued to walk until we got to the rock we had marked, walked down and finally got to the river beach.

We found the rafts that had survived the flood but some of the other things we had left there were gone, washed off by the water.

We started to take turns to navigate from one side to the other and, once we were all together on the other side, we organized the groups. Andy put Malagon on John's team and Carlos with Ben and Hans. He would continue with us and Luis.

We continued walking and John was ahead passing through the left gallery that would take us to our objective. He walked approximately 800 feet to find yet another gallery on the left. This gallery was higher so they had to use special equipment to climb to it.

Norman told the group that he would not be able to follow them. He said he would wait there, as he was too old and could not make the effort.

    —   OK – John said as he continued with Bill, Tommy & Malagon.

John looked at Norman and signaled him with five fingers and a wink (he was telling him that they had 5 hours to work).

They continued with the very dangerous climb, helping each other until they got to quite a large gallery that was positioned next to another gallery that sat on the east side of the main one.

After taking a short break, they saw Norman go down to the main level of the cavern and sat down on top of a rock.

Finally, John and his group got up and said goodbye to Norman as they continued walking to explore the gallery.

This gallery was full of stalactites and stalagmites and the floor had what seemed to be white fountains where drops of water would fall, making these formations even larger. Here you could tell that it had been a long time since the river had reached this level. Admiring the beauty of the place, they continued on.

After waiting just a couple of minutes, Norman got up and rapidly walked towards the ship.

After a half an hour of walking or better yet, running, he finally got to the ship where Charles and Jeff were waiting.

He went inside the ship immediately along with Jeff and started to use the equipment he had brought in what seemed to be a door. He positioned the computer with which he had been able to decode the combination to the entrance.

This time the computer was much faster, using the data saved from the previous entrance. The door opened slowly revealing a multitude of lights that continuously changed color, around what seemed to be a giant screen, which was not on.

Jeff and Norman couldn't believe their eyes.

- This seems to be a control cabin. – Said Jeff. – But everything is empty. What if someone actually drove this? How come there is no sign of anyone?

They went inside the main hall and began searching for any clues as Norman said:

- Don't touch anything, as we don't know what could happen!

After going around in circles, not finding anything, Norman took out a small camera and started taking pictures of everything.

When he took one of what seemed to be the giant screen, the flash revealed some strange signs on the actual screen.

Norman sat down to the right, trying to analyze the signs and connecting the other computer to the ship.

Looking at the lights in what seemed to be an instrument panel, he waved his hand over one of them that was lit and the light became even more intense.

The light went from red to blue and the screen was now much brighter.

There was a map with hundreds of stars and a run, he looked away and he observed what appeared to be a planet. Nelson took pictures of the map. He waved his hand over the light again and the planet became closer and closer until they could see green extensions of land, with water currents that crossed them.

Once again, his hand waved over the light and we could now see a city, buildings with architectonic lines very different from the ones on earth.

He moved again and a strange figure was revealed. It looked like a human being but wider with a much larger head and black, penetrating eyes. The figure was covered with what appeared to be a leather hat that went all the way down to its chest.

There were long and sharp upper extremities that ended with fine hands and extremely long fingers.

Everyone felt shivers when, all of a sudden they heard a fine voice with a soft, musical tone, speaking in an unknown language that not even the computer could decipher.

They were so shocked that nobody could even notice that Charles was yelling out at them!

Norman and Jeff were able to come out of their amazement first. Norman asked Charles:

   — What is wrong?

— It's time to go. It is already very late!

Norman got up and the screen automatically went blank.

They exited the ship and Norman started walking towards the meeting point.

After a half hour of fast walking or running, he got to the point just in time to see some lights on the upper gallery.

It was John and his group coming back.

Norman sat down for a minute. He was feeling extremely tired both physically and emotionally.

As John and his group approached, he could hear the laughter of the other group that was coming back from the main gallery: Miriam, Andy, Luis and I.

We got to the meeting point simultaneously and immediately got on our way back to the entrance of the cavern.

It was late when we got back to the campground. We all went to the river to bathe. The men went one way while Miriam and I went the opposite.

We felt much better as we went back to the main tent where a succulent meal awaited.

After some chit chat, we each went back to our own tents so we could lay down to rest.

John signaled me and I stopped by his tent.

There we also met with Norman who was still wide eyed as he explained what he had seen earlier.

Norman was desperate to go back.

- — Let's see if you can go back tomorrow – I said – But we need to be very careful so that nobody finds out.

After hearing his story and worried about this new encounter, it was very hard for me to fall asleep that night.

AUGUST 4TH

I saw the sun come up and realized I had not gotten much sleep thinking how we could get Norman to go back to his favorite place

I really couldn't figure out a way.

As we stepped out of our tent, we could see Norman carrying some bottles, a small jar and some other equipment, including a magnifying glass.

He looked like a real scientist.

- — What are you going to do? – I asked.

- — I'm going fishing. – He answered.

He was very serious and added:

- — I want to analyze the species at the entrance and around the cavern.

We got to the main tent where we were greeted for breakfast.

After eating, we started our walk towards the entrance of the cavern.

Once inside, we approached the collapsed rocks. Nelson said he was going to stay there looking for species. He claimed that would give him time to relax a bit, as he was too old for so much exercise.

Andy agreed and we all went towards the back of the cavern.

After crossing the river, we divided the group into three parts. We left Luis at the main meeting point with all the rafts. John left with Bill, Tommy and Carlos through the main gallery on their way to the second gallery.

Charles and Jeff, along with Malagon continued forward through the main gallery, followed by Miriam, Andy and myself.

We walked for about a half hour, and we finally reached a large gallery towards the left. We continued through that one while Charles, Jeff and Malagon kept on walking through the main one.

After a while, we found a fountain with many cave pearls. They were beautiful and very bright. The surroundings were also beautiful so we stopped to take some pictures.

We were enjoying the area and taking pictures while we spoke to John who had gotten to a junction that went up the cavern and that looked promising.

In order to save time, I told Tommy and Carlos to continue through the largest one (it seemed to be longer). They agreed to meet us at this same place in five hours.

Once on their way, they waited a couple of minutes and immediately started walking back towards the first gallery.

They ran so as not to lose any time. They were going east towards the gallery that John had discovered and that communicated with the cavern that held the missiles.

This time they stayed away from the edge so as not to be detected. John told Bill to look for the explosives they had left there and to get them ready.

Since he knew the place, he would be the one in charge to activate the detonators and to set them to allow for 8 hours before exploding so they could have enough time to escape.

They immediately started walking back to the meeting point.

Norman slipped away quietly from the cavern, and slowly walked towards the cave about 500 feet to the left of the riverbank. He went in and could hardly pull himself through until he reached the gallery and could stand up. He started running through the gallery on his way to the collapsed rocks.

Once there, he greeted Charles and Jeff and went inside the ship, asking them to call him in exactly three hours.

He sat right in front of the screen, started waving his hand on top of the instrument panel.

The giant screen started to come alive with lights that shimmered also in other areas of the cabin, displaying new blue maps. This time he was able to connect his computer with astronomical data, as he was obsessed with finding out where this ship had come from. (All the time, he kept blaming himself for not studying more Astronomy!!!)

Time flew and all of a sudden, he heard Charles' voice telling him:

— Drop it! It's time to go! It's late!

Not very happy but realizing he had to go, Norman got up, picked up a small CD and started on his way back.

He ran until he reached the very tight gallery where he had to pull through once more until he was able to reach the entrance.

He looked out, waited a few minutes while he gathered his strength, trying to hear if there was any activity in the surrounding areas.

Once he confirmed there was nobody around, he quietly slipped back to the entrance of the cavern.

Once there, he took off his boots and socks and went in the river with all the bottles he had brought in.

He was able to compose himself and started gathering some insects.

About an hour went by before he heard some voices. It was the rest of the group coming back.

I look at him and asked:

    — So, how was the fishing?

    — Not very well – He answered, smiling.

The rest of the group continued on while Miriam and I stayed behind to take a private bath.

Andy told us not to take too long so we could eat.

I agreed and, after taking a fast bath, we started walking towards the main campground.

As we got there, dinner was being served: Pork, Congris (rice & beans cooked together), sweet potato, bread and a few cold beers.

After dinner, we all sat down in front of a campfire to talk.

We had been chatting for a while when we heard a jeep approaching.

It reached the campground and some military men stepped out.

They asked Andy to one side and I heard him arguing with them.

A few minutes later, they went back in the jeep, shut the door and sped away.

- Is anything wrong? – I asked Andy.

- It seems there are problems with the military personnel. They told me to meet them at 9 AM tomorrow in Pinar del Rio. – He continued – I will start off early tomorrow on my way to the city. Hopefully I will be back in the afternoon and will let you know what happened. It is very probable that we will be asked to leave so try to explore the cavern in the morning but don't go too far out.

Andy went to sleep, as he had to get up early.

Miriam and I went back to our tent. I signaled John to come by.

After a few minutes, John was in out tent:

- What is going on? - He asked. – I didn't like the visit from the military. They did not look too happy.

- It seems there may be problems with us being here. They don't like us roaming around and, from what Andy told me, it is probable that they will ask us to leave.

- So then I am going to get a hold of the helicopters. – John said. –I will set everything up for tomorrow at midnight.

— That will be fine. – I said – Andy will be here tomorrow afternoon

— Andy will not be here in the morning so that will work in our favor. – John said – That will give us time for Norman to be at the ship and take all the pictures and information he can. We need to coordinate the groups. Bill has to come with me. Norman will go with Tommy, Carlos and you. Ben and Hans will go their way and will take Malagon. Miriam should say that she has a sprained ankle so that, once we cross the river, she can stay with Luis taking care of the rafts. – He continued with the specifics – We should all be back at the campground by 3 PM. We need to take longer picking up the material, as it is necessary that night falls as we are on the roadway to Sumidero.

It was then that Norman arrived, looking worried and said:

— I heard what you said John but I don't think I'm going to have time to decipher all of this. I need more time!

— I'm sorry – John said – We need to leave by 3 PM tomorrow. You must tell Charles and Jeff that they need to exit the cavern and hide near the campground by 4 PM. Regardless, I will speak to them tonight at midnight.

John turns to me and says:

— Is everything clear?

— Yes! – I answered while Norman was talking to himself.

John goes to find Tommy. He is going to have to work all night – I think – with radio communications.

I go back inside the tent. Miriam notices that I am worried and she asks why. I try to explain as much as I can without worrying her. I also tell her that tomorrow she needs to play a role like an actress – She needs to say that she has a sprained ankle so that Luis will stay with her and not join the group.

–   We are leaving. Try to sleep. Tomorrow is *the* day!

I go to bed but I just toss and turn. I cannot get any sleep and neither can Miriam.

All of a sudden, we feel the breeze and it starts raining over the campground.

This is all we need – I think – Let's hope it's over by morning.

I finally fell asleep after a while.

AUGUST 5TH

I awake to the noise of a motor.

I look at my watch – it is 5 AM and it seems it stopped raining.

I look out of the tent and I can see Andy along with someone. They are already on their way to the road.

The jeep is having problems with the mud. It moves slowly going South.

I can't go on sleeping. Miriam has not noticed anything.

I get up and go to the main tent where I see Cheo and Malagon talking.

— Good morning – I say to them.

— Good morning – They answer back. Cheo had just brewed some coffee and offered me some.

They asked why I was up so early. I told them the noise of the motor woke me up.

I went back to our tent. I walked in and sat down staring outside while I could feel the breeze on my face. I tried to think how this day may end. I was sorry that we couldn't finish the investigation on the ship. On the other hand, we had no other choice but to destroy it. Create a cave-in that would hide it forever.

I was also worried as to how we were going to escape, that is if we did not die trying or if we were not captured.

I thought about Miriam. Now I felt I shouldn't have brought her with me.

Thoughts were flying in my mind and tortured me while I could see the sun coming up. Slowly the night turned to day and the morning fog disappeared giving way to a very tropical sun.

The campground regained life. I could hear the guys' voices as they were getting up and the noise in the kitchen, where they were cooking and I started to smell the bacon and sausage being prepared.

Miriam finally woke up, she stretched, got close to me and looked in my eyes.

— Too early to rise. That just tells me that you are worried.

I guess we've been together for many years. It gets to a point where each one knows when something is wrong with the other or if there is a problem.

She didn't say anything else. She knew something was going on that worried me. She stepped away from the tent, went to the river to wash herself and then came back to me.

As a kitten she started to get close to me and smiling, she said:

- You need to smile – You are going to scare the guys or they will think something hurts.

- My heart hurts – I said. – It hurts me to have to do things that I don't agree with. Things that are against my principles, against science.

- Just remember that this is your doing, your idea, the only way to stop it from getting in the wrong hands. – She answered.

- You are right – I said, kissing her on the cheek. – You always have a way of enlightening the way. I don't know what I would do without your help.

I got up and grabbed her arm. We started to walk towards the main tent where the guys were already getting ready for breakfast.

John approached me, greeted us and started to devour breakfast much faster than normal. (I realized I was not the only one that was nervous)

So we all had a fast breakfast and started to gather our backpacks.

Carlos who, since Andy was not here, was acting a chief on the Cuban side looked at us and said:

- We need to leave so we can be back early. We must be here by the time Andy gets back. (This seemed like a confirmation that we needed to leave today).

I spoke to John and told him I had no doubt that we needed to go ahead with our plans.

John nodded his head and we all started walking towards the entrance to the cavern.

We went up the collapsed rocks at the entrance until we reached the main riverbank. We walked around the river until we reached the area of the cave-in, we climbed through the rocks until we reached the opening and then started walking back down to the river.

We got in the rafts so that we could meet on the other side and, all of a sudden, Miriam slipped, fell, and immediately started saying that her right ankle hurt.

I looked at her ankle and told her she had sprained it. I said she could not walk so she would have to stay.

— But... Do I need to stay here alone? – She asked.

Carlos looked at me and said:

— I'm sorry but if we are divided in three groups, you will have no other choice but to stay here alone.

Norman spoke up and said:

— I am probably the oldest and the one that is mostly tired, so I will stay with her.

I winked at Norman and told him to take good care of her.

We turned to Carlos and I asked if Hans and I could go with him through the main gallery. Ben and Tommy could follow us with Malagon as they were trying to reach Sumidero (Fuentes cavern entrance) . John and Bill could go with Luis to finish exploring the left gallery.

Carlos thought it was fine and, after saying goodbye to Miriam and Norman, we started walking.

A few minutes later, we reached the left gallery and, while John, Bill and Luis climbed up the walls, we continued on our way.

Ben, Tommy and Malagon went ahead of us as they had to get there sooner in order to achieve what they had set up to do.

Hans, Carlos and I continued walking for more than an hour until we got to a left gallery that we had already explored with Andy and where I wanted to take some pictures.

Once there, I took out the camera and began to examine the ammonites, and take pictures of the secondary formations. All of a sudden, I called Carlos and showed him a bone that sat on one of the rocks. I told him it belonged to some ancient creature but, because of its condition, it would be hard to determine the right species. I told him we would need to come back with some equipment in order to retrieve it.

While we were doing this, Norman left Miriam with a kerosene lamp and ran towards the ship.

He was sweating when he got there and greeted Jeff and Charles as he stepped in. Jeff told him they had received orders to leave the ship by 4 PM and that he (Norman) had to leave by 3 PM.

– OK – Norman said – As he entered the ship.

On the other side, John was walking through the gallery. They let Luis get ahead of them and told Bill to connect the detonators so that they would go off at 12 midnight. He warned him not to get close to the border and to get back as soon as he could.

— Meet me at the main gallery – John said – You will say that you walked through another gallery that went around and ended ahead.

— Ok – Bill said – And immediately started to walk back.

John took out his knife to mark a gallery that was to his right and immediately started to walk towards Luis.

He allowed Luis to continue ahead while he followed a few minutes behind. This went on for a couple of hours. They were crawling through very tight spaces until they finally got to a small area where they could stop to take a break.

Luis was asking where Bill was – He started to ask John in half English, half Spanish and with some sign language.

John tried to explain to him in English that he had stayed behind exploring a gallery and that they had agreed to meet later.

Luis did not like this and he signaled John to start walking back through the gallery.

John was closer to the gallery so he went in first. This would help him make the journey back much slower.

They started their way back as Luis, who was in back, complains constantly about how slow they were going.

Meanwhile, in the East Gallery, Bill was trying to set up the explosives.

He started to connect and hide them under some rocks. A rock suddenly became loose and rolled down. Bill couldn't do anything.

He stood still as he heard the rock fall and, after some very tense seconds, he could hear it land over some metallic surface.

A sharp alarm went off and it could be heard inside the whole cavern.

He finished hiding the explosives, he made sure there were no tracks left and he started to walk slowly at first and, after a couple of minutes, turned to a desperate run for his life.

He was able to get back faster than he thought. He climbed the gallery and ran to the place where they were supposed to meet. He could hear his heart pumping as he just leaned over the wall.

About a half hour later, John and Luis came out. They could tell that Luis was relieved to see Bill.

They all sat down to take a break and Bill told John that the gallery got too tight and that is why he decided to come back.

After a while, they started their way back and, approximately a half hour later, they got to Miriam.

Luis asked where Norman was. She didn't move an eye when she said:

- Norman was not feeling very well. He had an urgent need to relieve himself so he ran...I mean, he started swimming because he didn't want to take one of the rafts. He told me it would be faster if he swam.

Luis was not too convinced. He didn't say anything. He sat down and waited for the rest of the team.

About 45 minutes went by before they could see the lights coming back. Both groups had met inside, on their way to the exit and were talking.

When we got to the river, Carlos asked about Norman and Luis told him that he had not felt well and that he had left the cavern.

We started our way back on the rafts and then walked. We climbed through the collapsed rocks that would allow access to the entrance. We then walked down and could see the light, which guided us on the way out. We were very quiet and it was obvious that the Cubans did not like the fact that Norman had left.

Miriam was behind, next to me. She was faking a limp. We went down the riverbank and walked towards the campground.

As we were approaching the campground, something was happening inside the cavern around the ship.

Charles went inside the ship and could see Norman as he was talking to the giant screen.

- What are you doing? – Charles asked.

- I have been able to establish contact with them through the language computer. – Norman answered.

- So what are they saying? – Charles asked.

- Shut up! – Norman said – I am too busy with other important things now.

- They may be important things but you need to leave now. You are twenty minutes late!

- I know but I can't – Norman said.

- There is no excuse. Our orders are for you to leave and you must leave.

Norman was very upset. He hit the instrument panel and slowly started getting up, looking around as if saying goodbye to his surroundings. He looked at Charles who was standing next to the exit and said:

— Let's go!

Charles turned around, walked out and he could feel that Norman would have no other choice but to say goodbye. Suddenly, Norman threw his camera and a CD out towards Charles and then proceeded to close off the exit.

— Are you crazy? – Charles yelled – Open the exit way!

There was no answer.

Jeff approached and, looking at Charles, asked:

— What is going on?

— It is 3:30 and this guy refuses to leave. He closed off the exit way. – Charles answered.

— What are we going to do? – Jeff asked.

— We have ten minutes left to connect the explosives so they will go off at midnight – Charles said – And only twenty minutes to exit the cavern. And Norman knows we need to do this. This guy wants to be put to rest here!

— Let's get going – Jeff said as he picked up the camera and the CD – We have no time to lose. I hope he knows what he is doing and decides to exit before it's too late.

They started to move around the ship and the galleries surrounding it where they had hidden the explosive for the demolition.

They adjusted their watches and the clocks on the explosives so they would go off on time. They made sure that the clocks were set so as not to allow anyone to disconnect them. If they tried this, they would explode.

About fifteen minutes later they met at the gallery that would lead them to the exit. They started their walk out of the cavern.

It took them twenty minutes to reach the exit. Once there, they lowered themselves towards the valley and got on their way to the campground.

They were trying not to make any noise. Each one was carrying a backpack with guns. Jeff had a 9 Mm pistol while Charles had his 45. They also had an AK rifle on hand with enough ammunition.

They reached the closest place they could on the other side of the river. They sat down behind some trees and waited to hear instructions over the radio.

Charles kept looking towards the campground using binoculars. It started to rain.

- They are just getting there – He said to Jeff as he looked at his watch. – It is now 5 o'clock.

Back at the campground, John was one of the first ones to get there. He went inside his tent and immediately called Charles.

- Yes? – Charles answered.

- We have a problem – John said – Where is Norman?

- He didn't want to come back – Charles said.

There were a few seconds of silence.

- I'm on my way to get you – John said to Charles – Put on a raincoat that hides your head. Where exactly are you?

- On the other side of the river – Charles answered – Just west of the campground – Almost immediately in front of your tent.

- Don't move from there – John answered.

He exited his tent and went to the main tent where everyone was. I was just getting there with Miriam, who was limping. We were very wet from the rain.

Andy was there and frowning he asked:

- Where is Norman?

- He must be fertilizing the ground. He was not feeling well and had diarrhea. – I said.

- What are they saying? – John asked in English.

- They are asking about Norman – I answered.

- We need to pick up everyone's belongings – Andy said – I have orders from the military that we must leave, so start closing down your tents and you (looking at us) put your backpacks in the jeeps.

He looked at the Cubans and said:

- You are probably going to be delayed, so Carlos, Luis and Malagon stay with Cheo and the truck driver so you can help load the truck.

John looked at me and spoke in English:

— I am going to go looking for Norman.

I explained what we had said to Andy and immediately walked towards my tent with Miriam to pick up our belongings.

I could see John crossing the river and going into the jungle looking for Norman.

John arrived where Jeff and Charles were. He explained what they would have to do. Since Charles was more or less the same height as Norman, all he would need to do is cover himself well and not speak.

Jeff gave John a small nylon bag that contained the camera and the CD that Norman threw at them from the ship. John placed it in his pocket and started back with Charles on their way to the jeeps.

It was getting late and the rain just made everything darker. Night was rapidly approaching.

Andy kept yelling and screaming asking everyone to get going.

John went towards the last jeep and helped Norman climb in the back, where he laid down. I also saw John place a couple of backpacks on the jeep next to Norman. He closed the door and approached me.

— How is Norman? – I asked.

— I was able to fool everyone – He said – It is not Norman. He refused to exit.

— What? I said – Did they leave him behind?

— No! They did not leave him! – John said – He chose to stay and he knows the consequences. – He went on – Now go to the jeep and make it seem that you are giving him some medication and a blanket.

— OK – I said.

I went back inside my tent, then went by Norman's tent and picked up a blanket. I also got a small camera he had.

I went to the jeep under the rain and yelled out to Norman as I opened the door and got inside the jeep. When I lifted the raincoat, all I could see was the barrel of a 45 facing me.

— Just hide this Charles. – I said – I left the medication and covered him well with the blanket – Don't open your mouth! – I said.

I exited the jeep and went to the main tent. I could tell that Andy was following me with his eyes.

— How is he? - He asked me.

— He is weak because of the diarrhea. – I said – He told me he has not had any more bowel movements in the last couple of hours – I hope he is ok by the time we get to the hotel.

I sat next to him and asked:

— Why are they making us leave now? I thought they had approved our trip.

— These guys are very nervous – He answered – Remember that Vilma (the first lady) died in June and all the leaders are older than her. They are very old and fear they will die and the younger ones don't know what they are going to do when the older ones die. The only thing they think about is what is going to happen or who is going to lead the country. – I am really sorry that we could not go on but, in any event, you were able to spend enough time here.

It was almost 6 o'clock when John, noticing that it had gotten much darker, decided to call Jeff. He told him to cross now.

He walked with Ben and Hans towards the third jeep carrying some backpacks.

As they approached the jeep, they practically formed a barrier between men and backpacks in order to hide Jeff who climbed in the back of the jeep. They made sure he was ok in the back and then threw all their backpacks and blankets on top of him.

All three took a deep breath once they finished and, while Ben and Hans looked for their place in the jeep, the first one in the back seat and the second one in front, next to the driver. John walked back.

When he got to the main tent, which was still standing, he saw Bill and Tommy with their backpacks. They were on their way to the second jeep.

Once there, Bill opened the door and sat next to the driver while Tommy sat in the back seat.

At that time, Miriam came out of our tent. She was still limping and slowly walking towards the main tent.

    – About time! – I said – Women are always late!

    – And men always blame women! – Miriam answered.

Andy smiled and, after saying goodbye to the rest of the group, he called both drivers so they could take the second and third jeep. He was going to go on the first jeep and John, Miriam and I would go with him.

When he got to the jeep, he opened the back door for Miriam and me to get in. He then closed the door, sat on the front seat right next to Andy.

- Ready! – Andy said as he turned the key to start the jeep. He turned on the lights and started driving south towards the main road.

We were moving slowly and sinking in the mud.

Andy was saying that August was a bad month to explore caverns since it rains a lot – from August to October.

- The next time you should come anytime between November and February. – Andy said – Weather is better and there is not so much rain.

We continued slowly ahead on the mud-filled road, jumping up and down on the jeep until we got to the Guane highway.

As soon as we got to the highway, I asked Angel to stop so that I could stretch my legs and go to the bathroom.

- Are you sick like Norman? – He asked.

- Well....not that bad. – I answered.

- We'll stop at the exit of the town right next to a small stream.

- OK – I said.

We finally stopped where Andy had said. It looked like a good area. A lot of vegetation and as I stepped away from the jeep I could hear the stream.

— Do you want the guys to take the opportunity to answer nature's call? – I asked John.

I walked into the vegetation, I waited until John, Ben, and Tommy got there. The others were stretching their legs next to each jeep while they smoked a cigarette.

— This is it – John said – Let's take over. We'll tie them up and you – looking at me – give them something so that they will sleep for a few hours. – Try not to hurt them but do whatever you can so they don't yell – John continued – we are very close to San Carlos and someone could hear us.

We knew what we had to do and walked back to the jeeps. John went around the front and signaled that there was something wrong with the right front tire. Andy went around and looked at the tire but said he didn't see anything wrong. When he got up and turned around he was faced with a gun pointed at his head and, in perfect Spanish, John told him not to raise his voice or he would shoot him between the eyes. He ordered him to move towards the stream.

I was getting closer as Bill and Tommy were coming with one of the drivers who was scared stiff and kept asking them not to kill him.

A few seconds later Ben and Hans came carrying the other driver who was unconscious.

— What happened? – I asked.

— He fought back and there was no alternative but to *caress* him a little! – they said.

Andy looked at me in disbelief and asked:

— Why are you doing this?

— - Someday I will be able to tell you. – I said – But now it is impossible. All I will tell you is that you are going to sleep for about three hours. You will wake up at around 10:30 tonight. The ropes around you will not be too tight so you will be able to remove them from each other. – I continued talking to him – Just listen to me and listen well.....When you wake up and you leave, do not stop for anything until you get to Pinar del Rio. Do not lose time trying to let soldiers or the police know. Your life will be in danger. Once you are there, you can do whatever you feel is necessary. Some day you will realize why I said this and maybe, just maybe, we will see each other again.

We tied them up and got going. The night was darker than usual even though it was barely 7 o'clock.

John was driving the first jeep, Bill the second one and Ben the third.

They all started their jeeps at the same time, turned on the lights and started on their way to Sumidero.

I was sitting next to John and I asked:

— How are we doing with the gas?

— I think we're ok – John said – That is if the control panels on these jeeps work!

We got close to Sumidero. We could see some people walking, as we turned left on our way to the town of Gramales.

We were getting closer to the limits of the Pica Pica valley when a jeep with two men, dressed in military gear, stopped us and asked who we were and where we were going.

The first man approached John, but he didn't have a chance. John fired just one shot killing him while Jeff, who was in the second jeep, also fired, killing the second one.

We stepped out of the jeeps, pulled them off the road, and started driving as fast as we could.

— If anyone heard the shots, we would have all the military personnel following us in a few minutes. – I said.

Jeff and Charles had distributed the ammunition between them and signaled their lights. Bill approached us and gave us three AK rifles.

John turned off the lights of the jeep, waited until Bill and Ben got close to us and asked them to do the same.

We continued until we could see the town of Gramales, which looked quiet.

We could, however, see vehicles forming what seemed to be a barricade to close off the road and some shadowy figures moving around.

John was looking using the infrared binoculars and said:

— They are waiting for us. They know we are coming this way.

— What are we going to do? – I asked.

— I don't think there are too many of them – John said – Maybe four or six at the most.

We met in silence at the top of a hill right before the town.

John called Bill and spoke to him:

— You are the expert. Prepare a little gift that we can send ahead in one of the jeeps so that it opens the way for us. We will pick you up on the way.

A few minutes later, Bill had prepared a bomb and tied it to the bumper on his jeep, it would explode on contact.

Tommy and Jeff got in the jeep that John and I were in. I moved to the back seat with Miriam while Tommy sat next to John in the front seat. Jeff sat in the back seat with us, so Miriam was in the middle.

They moved the backpacks with the rest of the guns to the back of the jeep while in the other vehicle, Ben, Hans and Charles got ready.

Charles positioned a rifle in the trunk on back of the jeep and said:

— We're ready!

They would be the ones in charge of picking up Bill after he jumped out of his jeep.

— We are ready – John said – It's time to start the fireworks!

I looked at my watch, it was 8:30 PM.

Bill got in the jeep, the motor off and, after we helped push the vehicle down hill, he allowed the jeep to move towards the entrance of town.

About 200 feet before reaching the barricade, he tied the steering wheel and jumped out at more than 30 miles per hour.

After we pushed him downhill, we kept our jeeps off. Since we were far away, we could not see if Bill had already jumped but we could see that the jeep was moving along with no problem.

It was a few feet away when we heard rifles going off. We could see the lights of the shots hitting the jeep and, almost immediately, we heard a loud explosion. We saw the cars in the barricade as well as the soldiers as they were thrown into the air.

John started the jeep and sped downhill. We were able to go through the fire among the vehicles while we heard the shots from Tommy and Jeff's AK rifles.

After we went through Bill jumped in the other jeep which was following ours and, since nobody was expecting this, they were able to go through without firing one shot.

We were speeding as much as we could but we knew that the military would be on our backs in a matter of minutes.

We flew like a bullet next to a truck that was coming in the opposite direction but apparently, it was empty and had no military personnel on board.

A half hour went by of us speeding as much as we could. We finally reached the surroundings of the Sarmiento Farm.

We turned on the lights in order to go through the posts as if we were military personnel also. In these posts, the personnel did not have radio or phone, so we did not have to kill them.

We passed them without any problem and continued on our way to the Port of Santa Lucia.

We turned the jeep's lights off again and continued on our way.

When we were a half a mile from the town of Santa Lucia, we stopped to look through the binoculars. We could not see any apparent military movement.

The military office was dark. We knew that they only had a few men working there so we thought that, if they knew anything, they would be waiting for reinforcement.

We decided to keep the lights off and go pass it as fast as we could.

As it turned out, we were able to get through with no problem. We continued on our way to the bridge. John stopped and when the others stopped next to us, he told Bill to place some other *gifts* on the roadway.

He immediately continued our way towards the dock while Bill and Hans jumped from the jeep and placed some mines, the first ones were large and separated. The others were smaller but much closer to each other. When they finished, they got back on the jeep and followed us to the dock.

In the meantime, John had gotten to the dock but turned left in order to hide the jeep.

We all jumped off. Tommy started to cut some branches and throw them on top of the jeep while Jeff slowly moved to the place where he had hidden the rafts.

As soon as Ben, Hans, Charles and Bill got there, they parked next to the other jeep and proceeded to throw branches on top of it also.

John asked Tommy if they had been able to make contact. Tommy answered:

— Yes! They plan to meet us in approximately one hour, twelve miles from here. Let's walk so we can get under the dock.

Charles went first in order to help with the rafts. The meeting point was on the other side of the dock. He ran over silently, like a shadow in the night.

John looked at Miriam and me and said:

- You and Miriam try to take cover immediately under the dock. Don't lose any time!

It seemed easier said than done. We started running as if we were training for the Olympics. I could almost feel my boots hitting my back, but Miriam was going faster than me. I don't know if it was the terror she felt but I saw her run as never before in our lives together. We got to the dock and lowered ourselves, hiding among some tree trunks.

John had stayed behind organizing the getaway. His orders were heard:

- Ben and Hans, you will be in charge of making sure that this getaway goes the way we planned it. Make sure to put the rifles here to cover our way and then run to the dock as soon as we call for you. - John said - Make sure you are covered under the dock.

Looking at Bill, John added:

- Put all the ammunition you have left on the front of the dock. Do this after you are sure you have protected Ben and Hans' getaway.

We heard the sound of a helicopter approaching. It was still far away but we could hear it.

- We should have known this. - John said - I hope they can't see us. - He turned to Ben - Give me one of the bazookas. You keep the other one.

They moved away and tried to hide under the vegetation that surrounded them, as they could see a Russian helicopter approaching with search spotlights.

They tried to get as far away from the jeeps as they could. This was an excellent move as the pilots of the helicopter discovered the vehicles and opened fire with some missiles, destroying them instantly. The fire could be seen for miles.

The helicopter turned around and started firing shots with their rifles.

We could see the lights of at least four vehicles approaching.

    —   This does not look good. – John said – We are going to have to do something to end this situation.

The helicopter turned around and came really close to the group. At that precise moment, John used the bazooka and fired.

There was a huge explosion that made the night tremble while the helicopter was destroyed in small pieces.

    —   It's time to get going – John said as he, Tommy and Bill ran to the other side of the road and lowered themselves under the dock.

While all of this was going on, Miriam and I had reached the farthest part of the dock. We were under water, holding on to the tree trunks. I was holding on to the AK rifle so as not to lose it. We heard the explosion but didn't know what had happened.

The cold water, the uncertainty and the darkness of the night was overpowering. We had been in this position for a little over a half hour but it seemed it had been hours.

— Don't worry! – We heard John say – Charles and Jeff are on their way!

It was then that we heard an explosion.

— I think the little gifts we left them are starting to work! – John said.

We then heard Jeff's voice and we could hear him bringing the raft under the dock. A few feet behind, Charles was carrying the other raft. He was also taking refuge under the dock.

John called Ben and Hans and told them we were waiting for them.

We heard another explosion and immediately the sound of rifles going off.

— Who are they shooting at? – Tommy asked.

— I guess they are shooting at the shadows – John answered.

Ten minutes went by but it seemed like ten hours. Finally, the whole group was there.

— We have no time to lose. – John said – Get on the rafts.

Miriam, Tommy and I got on Jeff's first raft. We moved away from the dock in silence. We were rowing slowly. Charles, Ben, Hans and Bill followed us in the second raft. They carried a backpack and a rifle.

They tried to keep silent as they followed us. We were trying to hide as deep as we could on the floor of the raft. Jeff and Charles were the only ones rowing by now. Their outfits were black, just like the rafts. In the middle of this very dark night, we were hardly noticeable.

We could hear more explosions as well as the continuous fire of the rifles. It seemed they kept firing in the distance with no apparent target.

In the darkness of the night, our rafts moved slowly but steadily, taking us farther and farther away from the coast. Until finally we couldn't see it anymore.

Jeff stopped rowing and we could hear that Charles had done the same thing.

After a few minutes, John said:

— Turn on the motors!

Slowly, hardly emitting a sound, we moved into the sea traveling North. I looked at my watch. It was 11 o'clock but it seemed we had left the cavern a hundred years ago.

All of a sudden, we could see a light in the distance that was approaching us, illuminating the water.

— I think it is a Coast Guard boat – I said.

John said to stop the motors and we stayed adrift over the water.

We prepared our guns and rifles. Twenty minutes went by and we could still see the boat going around and around, trying to look for something in the sea.

In one of their last turns, the light made out Charles' raft and, automatically, the back and forth of rifles could be heard. The boat was much higher so their target was easy to see and the guys on it were good at shooting.

We were on the other side, covered by the darkness of the night and John picked up his AK rifle, along with Jeff and Tommy. I did the same thing and we all started shooting at the same time. The sound of the rifles being shot at the same time was extremely loud.

About five minutes later, the shooting stopped. We saw how the Coast Guard boat started sinking. John yelled:

—   Turn on the motors and let's go!

Everyone followed John's orders and the motors were now stronger than before. We were going North as we happily jumped up and down on the rafts, holding on to the ropes so as not to fall off.

We had been rapidly traveling North for about 15 minutes when John told us to stop.

We could hear the noise of potent motors far away and we saw lights reflected on the water. They were coming for us.

It was a speedboat driven by the military.

—   They are using all their resources – John said – They want to stop us no matter what.

He then turned to Charles and said:

—   Let's do this. Let's separate. You go North East and we will continue going North.

The motors were turned on and we were off again.

Once again, about five minutes into our journey, the speedboat detected Charles' raft and the sound of rifles back and forth could be heard.

John gave the order to keep on going – We were traveling North, parallel to the speedboat.

The guys in the speedboat did not notice that our raft was getting closer due to the intense sound of their own motors and the fire back and forth of the rifles.

John took out some grenades from his backpack. He gave one to Tommy and I was able to grab two.

— Let's see if I still remember my good old time playing baseball! – I said to John.

We were getting closer and closer. I looked at Miriam and I saw when she took Jeff's AK rifle. I smiled.

We were about a hundred feet from the speedboat when John yelled:

— Now!

All of us threw the grenades at the same time while Jeff sped away as fast as he could. John yelled again:

— Fire!

All four of us took out our AK rifles and began firing at the same time, surprising the men on the speedboat who were not expecting this.

We then saw how the grenades started going off. Two of them on the speedboat and two of them on the water.

There was fire everywhere and the wind was making it worse. Then, one final explosion was heard and the speedboat was completely destroyed.

We continued our way and reached Charles' raft.

- How are you? – John asked.

- Not bad. – Charles answered – One of the men is hurt.

- Who? – Asked John.

- It's Hans – Charles answered – Ben is helping him.

- OK – John said – let's continue North East as fast as we can.

Jeff sped away and we were followed by Charles' raft.

For the first time John turned to Miriam:

- I must congratulate you – He said – You were great! I didn't know you could handle an AK rifle.

- Pastor used to take me to practice – She answered – He always told me you need to be ready for any situation.

We all laughed.

We continued traveling with no problem for the next fifteen minutes. Then John asked us to stop again.

We waited a few minutes. Charles got close to our raft.

- What is going on? – I asked John.

- Charles' raft is taking water. It seems one of the shots damaged it and at the speed we are traveling, it tore even more.

John told them to throw all their ammunition out and ordered everyone to get their lifesavers on. Then all of them climbed onto our raft.

Hans had a lot of difficulty in the maneuver, due to the bullet lodged on his left arm. We all tried to help.

Once we were all together – we felt like sardines in a can – we continued our way but we had to move much slower as we were worried we would not make it if we went faster.

A half hour went by and then we noticed that our raft was taking water.

–   Too much weight – John said to Tommy – Send an SOS Light or we will not make it.

–   I already did – Tommy said – And I have contacted the helicopters but it takes them some time.

The water kept rising even though we were throwing it overboard constantly.

I looked at my watch and told John:

–   It is almost midnight.

I had not even finished uttering my words when, far away, we saw the sky light up with what seemed to be a nuclear explosion.

From within the explosion, we were able to see a very bright white light that went up to the sky and traveled into infinity.

–   What was that? – John said.

–   That was Norman – I said – He was able to do it! He managed to save the ship!

–   Or the ship saved him – John answered – Will we ever see him again?

> — Who knows – I said – With someone as crazy as he is, anything is possible.

AUGUST 6TH

12:30 AM

We are at a point that we can hardly keep on going. We are almost under water even though we threw away the motor.

All of us are shivering from the cold. It looks like we won't be able to make it.

Miriam is holding on to me, shivering and crying. This breaks my heart. I try to get her spirits high, I take her hands and try to warm them but everything is in vain.

A few minutes later, she starts throwing up. She tells me she feels very bad and I try to explain that it is due to the movement of the raft. She gets worse and seems to faint.

At that moment, we crashed into something hard.

> — Who is it? – We hear someone say in Spanish.

> — We need help! – I replied.

We boarded the small boat. It is made out of wood and must be 15 ft at the most. There is only one man on board.

> — Are you a fisherman? – I ask

> — No! – He responds. This is my third time trying to reach the US.

125

- Thank you for saving us – I say as John helps me lay Miriam down. I take out my first aid kid and give her a stimulant.

- So how do you move? – John asks.

- I have two rows and a sail. – He answers.

- Our motor broke yesterday. Let's take turns rowing – John continues – We need to move as much as we can before dawn breaks.

We continued rowing all night.

- What's your name? – I ask the Cuban.

- Jesus – He answers – I am from Mariel. I have been trying for years to escape from the island but the two previous times the guards caught me and put me in jail. I have no family in the Yuma (US), so I have no other choice but to risk drowning in order to get there.

- We are about 12 miles from the coast – John interrupts – but that is not enough. We have to keep moving away

It is 5:30 AM and we can see some light starting to rise from the East. Daytime is near.

The sun finally comes up and while we were so desperate to see it, now it starts slowly burning us.

It is now 9 o'clock in the morning and we continue our way with the homemade sail.

We can see a cargo ship ahead but because of the direction it is going, we don't even attempt to get their attention.

We continue on, it is now 11 in the morning, and there is no sign of the helicopters.

At about I PM we finally see a helicopter on the North side.

Tommy tries to get the helicopter on the radio. He thinks it's them!

We see a Russian MIG flying at a high altitude. They get close to the helicopter that now turns left and starts off towards the East, apparently trying to distract them so they won't see us.

Tommy tells John that the helicopter radioed Homestead Air force Base.

Less than five minutes later, we see two American jets get close to the MIG as it turns back rapidly and starts going South.

– Amazing how fast they can do this – I tell John.

– Those two were already in the air when the helicopter pilot got a hold of them. They were waiting. – John answers.

Ten minutes go by and we see the helicopter get close to us. I can't describe the feeling as we saw it approaching. It threw down a basket and we all started climbing. Miriam was first, then me and then John, Hans & Tommy.

Then we saw another helicopter. We got away from the boat and started on our way back.

The others started climbing the second helicopter. First, the Cuban raft man, then Bill, Charles, Ben & Jeff.

Now that we feel more at ease, I tell John I can't wait any longer. I open my shorts and get my Money Bag out. I open it and take a nylon sac out. I open this sac and pull another nylon envelope.

— I'm glad I was careful when I hid this. – I say – If not, it could have been lost with all the water!

I finally took out the envelope that Lieutenant Lazaro had given me. I started reading it, allowing enough space for John to see it too, as the noise of the helicopter did not allow me to read it aloud.

The first thing I see is a small paper written in ink that says:

"The papers that have been written on a typewriter are the Last Will and Testament of the Maximum Leader. This is written in three parts. One part is political and two parts are military. The military parts are 1 and then 2 in the event the first one fails. The ones in charge of following these orders are specific officials that have joined together in a brotherhood in order to make sure to follow the orders step by step. Their names have not been revealed."

"The following pages are copies of the Military – Part 1"

THE LAST WILL &
TESTAMENT

The first part starts:

Since our objective has been to destroy Imperialism and I have not been able to do it in my lifetime, I want to give my troops specific orders for their final battle.

We have been preparing for this moment for years. This is the moment where Communism will triumph.

The first step is to start a battle of the press, accusing them of wanting to destroy the Revolution.

Immediately after, we will start an invasion of rafters from Pinar del Rio thru Las Villas, sending a half a million in a mass exodus that they will not be able to stop.

Along with all the people, we will send hundreds of men that have been trained in demolition. Our agents in the US will be waiting for them at different points, including California and Florida.

These men will be in charge of demolishing all the important bridges, highways and train routes.

The objective will be to paralyze transportation. We need to do highways 10, 40, 70 and 80. These run from East/West. Then 95, 75, 55 and 25 which run North/South. All these demolitions will be coordinated with the attack of our planes.

As soon as we start the massive exit of rafters, the US will say that we have started an act of war for having allowed the exodus. In retaliation, they will probably attack our military stations.

We will be waiting for them.

Point number two will be to send transport planes of different nationalities, full of bacteriological warfare. These will explode above Washington, Chicago and California. These are key points so that the wind will distribute the contents throughout the US. That is why we have spent years manufacturing these special weapons and bombs. We have millions of them ready to go.

This will not be all. At the same time that the other planes are completing their mission, other commercial planes carrying potent explosives instead of passengers, will be in charge of destroying the Empire State. That is one building I hate because I feel it represents the Imperialists. Other planes will destroy electric plants, levis and some of their nuclear stations.

The pilots have already been trained. They come from Saudi Arabia, Afghanistan and Iraq. Our Jihad friends, who are very willing to complete this mission that we have all been preparing for.

Our South American friends will provide the planes, we will change pilots here and then they will fly to the Bahamas and to the South of Nicaragua. From here, they will depart on their way to the West Coast of the US.

The attacks of the planes must be simultaneous and they must be set at a specific time in all time zones. The first ones that should depart are the ones stationed in Nicaragua. The first three will fly to Washington, which is the farthest point. Then the ones for Oregon and lastly, the two that will fly to California.

The five planes that will leave from here with a stop over at the Bahamas will all carry very potent explosives. The first two will fly to New York to destroy the Empire State and the one to Washington D.C. will fly directly to the White House. The other three will take care of the specific nuclear plants in Ohio, Texas and Illinois.

We will finish our mission by using six bags that contain small nuclear bombs. We have been saving them and we will use them.

The first one will serve as the signal to start the total chaos, which will explode in the Plaza de la Revolucion during a massive demonstration where people will protest the attacks of the US on our military bases. In this explosion approximately ¼ of a million people will die. They will become ¼ of a million martyrs that perished defending the Revolution and will serve to accuse the Imperialists in front of the World for this massacre.

The press, which is our best ally, will be the best weapon throughout the capitalists countries of the World. They will take care of promoting the images of the explosion and that massacre will enrage the World against the Imperialists.

Our agents throughout the World will then take care of organizing attacks to all of the US embassies.

The Jihad will increase their movements within Iraq, Afghanistan and against Israel.

This will be the beginning of the greatest battle of all, the other five bags will be placed in various key points in the US. They should include Miami, New York, Atlanta and Detroit. They should go off the day after the attack of the planes with explosives and bacteriological warfare.

These are my last words in this, my Last Will and Testament. Until Victory as always, etc.

We were astonished.

- Well, we ruined one part of his plans, we just destroyed the bacteriological material – I said to John.

- And maybe even the second part also – John answered – by now, everything should be at CIA headquarters. We shall see what they say when they see the plans of this crazy devil incarnate.

- So what do you think about Lt. Lazaro? – I ask.

- I have no doubts that he was part of the preparations. He must be a member of the elite and all of a sudden realized that it was crazy and decided to save himself and his family. – John said – But I think we need to investigate him much more.

We were getting closer to the airport when I turned around to look at John and said:

- I hope they don't send the rafter back. Remember he was the one that saved us!

- Of course – John said – Don't worry about it. I will take care of it.

When we landed at Homestead Air force Base, there was an ambulance waiting.

They brought Hans down first, placed him in the ambulance and took him to the hospital.

Miriam, John, Tommy and I were helped down afterwards. We walked over to some military vehicles where there were some official personnel waiting for us.

We saw how John gave his military salute to them and identified himself.

- Yes, I know – the Lt. Said – Get in, they are waiting for us at the main building.

We finally reached the building and as we went pass one of the television sets, we heard the news: Cuba was accusing the US of a terrorist attack by mercenaries that destroyed a Health Department manufacturing plant of special vaccines for their citizens. They also said that because of the attack, more than a hundred thousand people had to be evacuated from the Pinar del Rio province.

John told me we should wait inside one of the rooms while he worked out some details. He followed the other officials into an office and closed the door. All three of us stayed back.

We sat down to watch TV and a woman, dressed in military clothes, approached us and asked if we wanted anything to drink.

- A soda please! – We all answered.

She came back a few minutes later with three very cold soda cans.

We thanked her, as we were very thirsty.

About an hour later, John came back. We were still savoring our sodas.

- Hey Doc – John said – They want you in Washington. The Department of State as well as the CIA wants to talk to you. I also have to go. Everything points to the fact that you probably will not have much time in the near future to work in your office. As a matter of fact, I think you should sell it!

- Why? – I said.

- Well, according to the Cuban Government we will be labeled as "Terrorists" and the US government wants to keep us guarded somewhere. They also want you to work with them

133

in various projects identifying other key points you may know. Welcome to the team!

Miriam looked at me and said:

—   I just want a small farm where I can take care of the plants!

—   Ok! – I said as we started to follow John on our way to some unknown future.

As we continued to walk, John turned around and said:

—   By the way, Lazaro was picked up and the other three "packages" were Miriam's sister, her husband and the contact called Pepe.

Miriam smiled and so did I. At least the family was safe.

We exited the airport's main building and they placed us in dark cars with tinted Windows.

We drove straight to the Miami Airport. They drove in through a side door that I didn't even know existed and drove into a hangar.

There was a plane waiting for us. We went up the escalator and sat in very comfortable leather seats. Then we heard the sound of the door being shut. I turned to John:

—   It looks like this is going to be a direct flight.

—   Yes it is! – John said.

I looked out the window and felt Miriam's hand squeezing mine as we took off.

All I could do was think: Goodbye Miami!

THE FUENTES CAVERN

PINAR DEL RIO SKETCH MADE BETWEEN 1965 & 1967
BY FERNANDO JIMENEZ & PASTOR TORRES

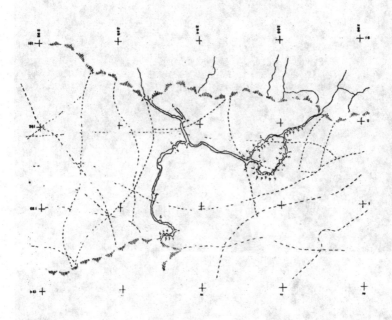

S I M B O L O S

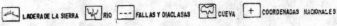 LADERA DE LA SIERRA RIO --- FALLAS Y DIACLASAS CUEVA + COORDENADAS NACIONALES

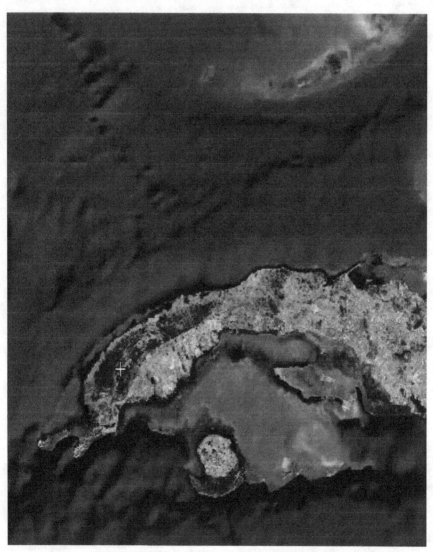

AREA OF EXPLORATION IN PINAR DEL RIO PROVINCE.

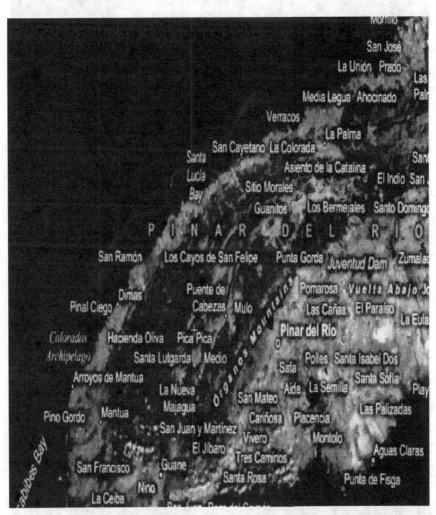

PINAR DEL RIO PROVINCE. PICA PICA VALLEY, SUMIDERO.

FUENTES CAVERN
PIO DOMINGO CAVERN
HOYO DE POTRERITO

FUENTES CAVERN RIVER BANK

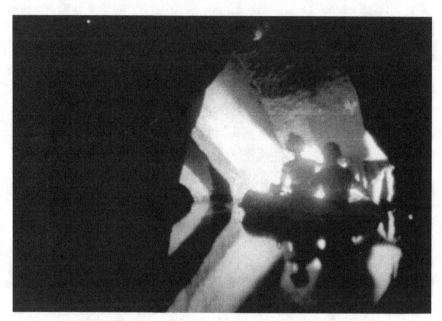

FUENTES CAVERN – SUBTERRANEAN RIVER

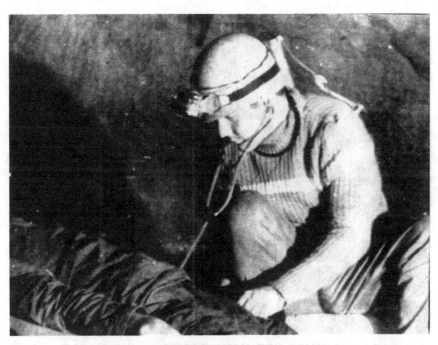

THE AUTHOR DURING ONE OF THE
EXPLORATIONS OF THE FUENTES CAVERN

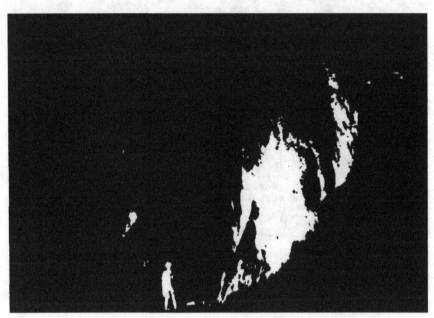

MAIN RIVER BED INSIDE FUENTES CAVERN

SUBRIVER BED INSIDE FUENTES CAVERN

PIO DOMINGO CAVERN, PICA PICA
VALLEY – MILITARY ZONE

PIO DOMINGO CAVERN

PIO DOMINGO CAVERN BEFORE THE
MILITARY CONSTRUCTION

THE AUTHOR TO THE LEFT WITH THE SPELUNKER
ALBERTO IGLESIAS IN THE PICA PICA VALLEY

SKELETON OF MEGALOCNUS RODENS
IN SITU PIO DOMINGO CAVERN

SOTERRANEOS CAVERN BETWEEN THE WINDOW
CAVE AND PIO DOMINGO CAVERN

PIO DOMINGO CAVERN

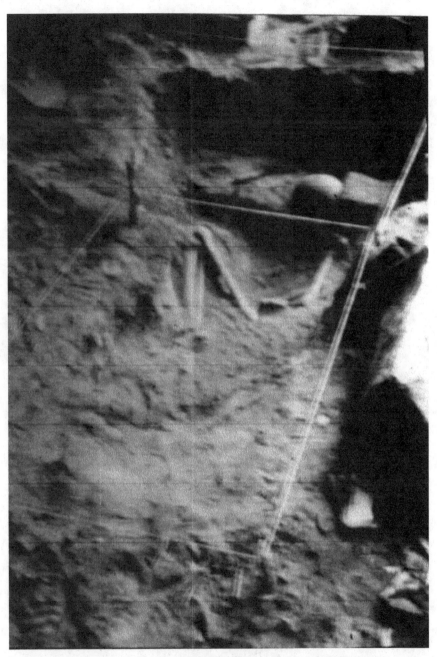

HUMAN REMAINS IN THE ARCHEOLOGICAL
EXCAVATION PIO DOMINGO CAVERN

Printed in the United States
by Baker & Taylor Publisher Services